Someone else

Someone else

Fictional essays **John Hughes**

First published 2007
for the Writing & Society Research Group
at the University of Western Sydney
by the Giramondo Publishing Company
PO Box 752
Artarmon NSW 1570 Australia
www.giramondopublishing.com

Designed by Harry Williamson
Typeset by Andrew Davies
in 10pt Baskerville

Printed and bound by Southwood Press
Distributed in Australia by Tower Books

National Library of Australia
Cataloguing-in-Publication data:

Hughes, John 1961–
Someone else: fictional essays

ISBN 978 1 920882 25 9

1. Essays. I. Title.

A824.92

for Mary Ann

Also by John Hughes

The Idea of Home

When I see such things, I'm no longer sure
that what's important
is more important than what's not.

WISLAWA SZYMBORSKA

Je est un autre

ARTHUR RIMBAUD

Contents

Preface

The story of a life should contain many puzzles and leave much to guesswork.
Some things should be presented in such a way that their nature is always
concealed. The story of a life is as secret as life itself. A life that can be
explained is no life at all.
ELIAS CANETTI

On a brief trip he made to Australia in his later years, when he
was by that time very ill, Max Brod had a conversation with a
young man he met in a small café by the sea. The man had no
shoes, Brod noted, and long hair which he kept in place with
a headband. He walked with a stoop, and even in the salty
heat wore an old ski jumper with holes in both elbows, worn
to threads at the sleeves. The man troubled the ageing Brod
who made in his diary over the next few months a number of
observations concerning their conversation, which, incident-
ally, went on for many hours. The man told Brod he felt there
was something wrong inside, he found himself translating all
the time, but without a change of language. 'I told him,' Brod
writes, 'that many people feel foreign in their own tongue.'
He seemed to like this idea because he gave Brod a menu on
the back of which he had written the following:

A good translation is a fire that leaves, like ash in the
new language, a trace of the original. It creates a kind of
language, a *style*, that has not existed until that moment
and could not be created *ab ovum* by a writer. Every word
in a good translation is like an echo, a shadow that is also,
somehow, the light that throws it.

Brod writes that the man was obsessed with Paul Celan who, he claimed, spent his whole life trying to translate his poetry from German into German. 'It's not just that I feel a stranger in my own language,' he told Brod, 'I'm not even at home in my imagination. My memory is not my own. Too many others have preceded me there...'

'With that he fell silent for some time,' Brod writes. 'I don't think he would have spoken again. It was as if he were being pressed down by some invisible force, but I was intrigued, and by seeming to steer our conversation down a different path, I gradually drew him out. He told me he had been overwhelmed by the thought that a writer's life cannot be anything other than a lived fiction, and that what the writer must strive for is a symbolic representation of his life and not be diverted by historical exactitude or the illusion of life as lived. Every writer leaves two works, he said, the written work and the image of himself, and both creations pursue one another till the end. He related to me a strange parable which I have not been able to forget, so vivid was the impression it made on me as the afternoon light faded quickly, as it does over here, and the air seemed to cool, and I was disturbed by the sound of the sea. This is what he said:

Imagine a book on the shores of a lake. A reader, coming across it, sees two books: one on the bank above the lake, and the other reflected upside down. Nothing exists or happens in the one book that the other does not repeat, because the book is so written that every detail will be reflected in its mirror image, and thus the book in the water contains not only all the words and punctuation marks of the book on the land, but also every nuance that might live in the gaps between them. The book's readers know that each of their actions is, at once, that action and its mirror image, which possesses the special dignity of images, and this awareness protects them against forgetfulness. Even when readers lose concentration, or engage in fanciful interpretations or connections with the world outside the book, it is not so much their daydreaming or flights of fancy that matter as the daydreaming or flights of fancy of the images, limpid and cold in the mirror. At times the mirror increases a word's value, at times denies it. Not all words that seem valuable above the water maintain their force when mirrored. The twin books are not equal, because nothing that exists or happens in them is symmetrical: every sentence and chapter is answered, from the mirror, by a sentence and chapter inverted, point by point. The two books live for each other, but there is no love between them.

He wanted me to understand that he was talking about himself here, though he wasn't clear which book represented him – I think he saw himself in both. What made the imagination so attractive, he said, was also what made it dangerous. Like the lovers on Keats's Grecian urn, frozen in the moment before consummation. He recited the whole poem for me then, quietly but without self-consciousness. The café was almost empty by this time, it was dark now, and the sea had grown louder. The woman behind the counter watched us but made no sign that she wanted us to leave. When he had finished the poem he stopped in a way that made me feel he wasn't finished but rather drawing breath, and that there was still one thing, perhaps the hardest thing, that needed to be said. He stared through the open door, as if the words he wanted were not to be found in his memory but playing themselves out there in the dark before his eyes. Bold lover, he said at last, I can never get past these lines,

Bold lover, never, never canst thou kiss
Though winning near the goal – yet do not grieve;
She cannot fade, though thou hast not thy bliss,
For ever wilt thou love, and she be fair!

What torture is unrequited desire, he said, but the moment the lover moves his blood begins to flow, he lets in life, he tastes those lips, and he will die. I don't think he cared if I heard him or not. Reading is the same, he said.

'I told him nothing of my own life,' Brod continues almost a week later, 'but I asked him if he had tried writing any of this down. Again he took some time to formulate his response, but I was growing used to his manner by now. Nevertheless, when finally he spoke, it was not as I expected. There are two ways to write a life like mine, he said, to write about others, I mean, because what else is my life but a kind of *unfolding*? He stressed the word.

A bud unfolds into a blossom but the flower which one teaches children to make by folding paper unfolds into a flat sheet of paper. This second kind of unfolding is the way a biographer approaches life. When he saw that I seemed puzzled by his analogy, he did not return, as I had hoped, to the first kind of unfolding, the one that truly interested me, but told me instead that as a young man he saw himself in all that he read. It was as if I had created a novel in my head, he said, the characters would not be still, they rose up from the pages of their different books and argued and fought and merged and grew inside me, but with an autonomy that made them as real to me as you are, sitting here now. I was not alone in this, he continued, everyone I knew at the time seemed to be acting out some kind of fantasy, but in the intensity of my imaginative identification, an intensity fuelled by the almost febrile world of the works themselves, and the way in which I viewed myself and the world around me almost entirely *through* these works, I was, perhaps, a little more extreme, a little more *possessed*. I wanted to be haunted. In my imagination I was a character that Beckett or Chekhov had created, I lived in their works as their characters lived in me...'

Brod's diary breaks off here, and he doesn't take up this conversation again for another ten days. But it seems to haunt all the other entries in between, and when he begins again it is as if continuing naturally from something he has written only a moment before. 'Would it surprise you, I said to him, if I told you that all our lives are made up of the lives of others? At this he almost smiled, the way melancholics or those suffering from severe accidie often do to humour or indulge their interlocutor. The dead annex the living, who become their replicas and successors, he said, the continuators of their interrupted life. Then write in this way, I started, suddenly impatient, as if in a reverie or dream…If ever I were to write about myself, he interrupted me, smiling as before, his words for the first time in a rush, you are right in this, it would have to be in this way, a trace rather than an image, what remains in me, a kind of growth, in the way a shadow is a growth. I could write about these figures who inhabit my imagination as surely as you inhabit my field of vision now, and although impossible, because dreams know no limit, I could, through careful study, become Proust or Mandelstam or Montale – but where would the interest be in that? And such an achievement would not capture my state in any case. He went on to say to me,' Brod writes, 'that to be, in some way, Mark Rothko, and to paint his paintings seemed less arduous to him – and, consequently, less interesting – than to go on being himself and arrive at Rothko's paintings through his own experience. The only way he could tell the stories of the figures in his head was by making them tell his stories; to create again what was already there by creating something new. And how could anyone do this, he asked, transform taking into a gift? One would have to conceive of a vampire, drinking his own blood…'

This time there is a gap of over two weeks, and when

Brod finally returns to the conversation it is for the last time, and we can sense the weariness in his voice. No one knew better than he how even the imagination must age, and he was, by this time, though he did not know it yet, only one week away from his death. 'When I suggested to him that all men are burdened by the terrible weight of influence,' he writes, 'and spend their lives searching endlessly (and fruitlessly, I added) for the freedom of some new form, I knew then that I had gone too far. But I felt compelled now to make him see. When Ch'ui the draftsman, I told him, in one of the stories of Chuang Tzu, is asked how he is able to draw more perfect circles freehand than with a compass, how his fingers can bring forth spontaneous forms from nowhere, he replies: When the shoe fits the foot is forgotten. But how can I put these reveries of mine into words when they are already words? he demanded. He mentioned then Wittgenstein's famous remark that had come to haunt him more than any other: 'If a lion could talk, we could not understand him.' He understood Wittgenstein to mean that it's not simply that we don't have words for certain states or feelings or experiences or apprehensions, if that were the case we could simply create new words. The problem, he said, was that some apprehensions simply cannot be put into words (he wanted to make it clear he was not talking about God here, what he was saying had nothing to do with mysticism), cannot really be thought about. He was talking about translation again, only in his case, he said, he had come to realise that the lion was not outside himself, existing independently of him, as Wittgenstein had observed, but was there inside his own head.'

Brod had been dead for thirteen years when this diary appeared. Even so, because I was drawn to the man and his misfortune, my first response was a feeling of awkwardness and embarrassment, I felt as if I was intruding precisely where I should not. But despite my embarrassment, I found these entries more absorbing than any literary work I had read for years past. Though brief, they are similar to those singular memoirs or collections of letters from which Brod himself drew sustenance. With reverence his loftiest feature, Brod had no qualms about reading, over and over again, the letters of Kleist, of Flaubert, and of Hebbel. For my part, I can only say these accounts of his conversations with the young man in the café have penetrated me like an actual life, and they are now so enigmatic and familiar to me that it seems they have been mental possessions of mine from the moment when I first began to accommodate human beings entirely in my mind, in order to arrive, time and again, at a fresh understanding of them. The penultimate entry for 1978 – coming late in the day, one might say – contains the following statement: 'I haven't yet written down the decisive thing, I am still going in two directions. The work awaiting me is enormous.'

J.H., Coogee, 2006

THINGS

The world is the totality of facts, not of things

ITALO CALVINO

THE BOOK THAT IS NO BOOK

Those who arrive at the house of the scribes can see little of this book beyond the stone walls, the sackcloth screens, the scaffolding, the metal armatures, the wooden catwalks hanging from ropes or supported by sawhorses, the ladders, the trestles. If you ask, 'Why is the book's construction taking such a long time?' the scribes continue hoisting sacks, lowering leaded strings, moving long brushes up and down, as they answer, 'So that its destruction cannot begin.' And if asked whether they fear that, once the scaffolding is removed, the book may begin to crumble and fall to pieces, they add hastily, in a whisper, 'Not only the book.' If, dissatisfied with the answer, someone puts his eye to a crack in the wall, he sees cranes pulling up other cranes, scaffolding that embraces other scaffolding, beams that prop up other beams. 'What meaning does your construction have?' he asks. 'What is the aim of a book under construction unless it is a book? Where is the plan you are following, the blueprint?' 'We will show it to you as soon as the working day is over; we cannot interrupt our work now,' the scribes answer. 'Work stops at sunset.' Darkness falls over the house of the scribes. The sky is filled with stars. 'There is the blueprint,' they say.

THE BOOK OF VANITY

You can still hear stories of a time before the One Book. Some say there might even have been thousands of books. It is impossible, but you can hear such stories often enough to convince yourself that it might be true. Even if there were just one other, what consolation! One might speak of a world then, the word *world* might actually mean something. All words might mean something, stand for something other than themselves, for the words that were this other book, the world that was this other book. But alas, if such a journey were possible once, it is conceivable now only in dreams, or the memories of the old men who tell the stories and will soon be no more. I do not mean to sound ungrateful. I know that for centuries my ancestors laboured with a faith that defies comprehension to reach an end – you need only read, it is all there in the book. Filling all the pages first – no one has ever been able to count how many – and then, when all hope seemed lost, when no page remained yet there were still more words, devising the brilliant solution of accretion, so that every page could be added to by fixing another to its margin, and when all these too had been filled, fixing yet other pages to them, so that the book, like their memories, might expand to fill the world, the words, in the end, more real than anything that might have preceded them. I know all this for I too (like you) am an inhabitant of the book. And if there is any hope for me, if there is any dream that comes to me at night, unbiddable, like grace, it is the thought that one thing, one tiny thing, has eluded the book. Can you tell me that I am wrong?

THE BOOK LIKE A FENCE

It exists only in parts, and never in one place. One needs to imagine it strung out in a line, a single sentence unrolled across the mountains and the plains, the deserts and the seas, the edges of the earth, unfurling, without end, past moon and sun and stars. How did it come to this? Imagine a book with catches like barbs that caught as it grew all earthly marks: algae traces on mangrove trunks; marine worm engravings on bark hulls and temple columns; bird prints, rock-pool whorls, tidal stains, tree weepings, dirt shadows, songlines of the restless spheres. To read one must walk and run and swim and fly, but following, always following this one line, now thin, now thick, now clean, now broken, tight, loose, heavy, light, feathered, dotted, smudged, bold and faded, curved and arabesqued, at once spearhead, smoke wisp, whip-crack, milky way, now worm line, now hook, now cuneiform, rune, hieroglyph, symbol, alphabet of the stars – Babel in one voice. An elusive book, no man who set out to read it has ever returned. And so, over the centuries, the legend has grown that language, too, is a fence. But what it is keeping out, or in, only one returning might know.

SOUTH

Like the beautiful bodies of those who died before they had aged,
Sadly shut away in a sumptuous mausoleum,
Roses by the head, jasmine at the feet —
So appear the longings that have passed
Without being satisfied, not one of them granted
A night of sensual pleasure, or one of its radiant mornings.

CONSTANTINE CAVAFY, 1904

He looked up at the small clock on the wall behind the bar. The young man had not said that he would come, yet the turn of his head when there had been no need to look back had been a kind of promise. *Until you did not come I did not know the pleasure of waiting.* The line had returned to him while reading Herodotus and he repeated it before finishing his coffee. Cold now. The story of Candaules, king of Sardis, and Gyges. Poor Candaules. Outside the day had turned grey and on the air faintnesses of the sea and the distant shrieks of gulls. He could just make out the Ministry of Public Works where he had worked for twelve years as a clerk in the Irrigation Service. In this poor leftover of a city.

At the table opposite the men were playing cards.

They played noisily, as if the noise itself were the point of the game, and he watched them for some time before he got up to join them. He played most evenings and knew all the faces. He removed a leather billfold from his trouser pocket and counted out the notes. He talked while he played, mainly about horses, and what had been won and lost. Caligula, he told them, put his horse in the Senate. As if it were yesterday. They referred to him as *Il Libro*, the walking book. Boredom, he told them.

At night he would close the shutters of his study and he would read. It was a kind of penance. Even thought was a form of punishment. He thought again of Herodotus. Of Candaules contriving the means whereby Gyges might behold his wife naked because he was convinced that his bodyguard did not believe his wife was as beautiful as he claimed. And Gyges, appalled by shame, yet unable to resist his master. He beheld her that night, undressing in her bedchamber, but she saw him and her husband too. And though she made no sign that night, she summoned Gyges the following morning and offered him a terrible choice. *Either slay Candaules and take me and the throne of Lydia for your own, or die this moment in his room.*

He had realised early that guilt was the form religion took in a non-believer's life. Walls of books. Julian the Apostate, heavy in his lap. The end of Greece was not Rome but rather the *end* of Rome – the words of a young God who would permit of no other god but himself. Later, he would walk through the leftover streets to the harbour. There were lights here and there on the water, lights in the bars, and buildings, older in their shadows. Older, even, than the words that came to him now from the books that would not be still, ghosts from beneath the sea. And the men who called them to their beds.

Your footsteps
Like water on stone.
If I had spoken yesterday
I would have missed their beauty.

(1904)

BETWEEN
(Two Parables
without a Message)

Oh, plenty of hope, an infinite amount of hope — but not for us

FRANZ KAFKA

1.

And it came to pass that God tempted Abraham. 'Take now your son,' he said, 'your only son Isaac, whom you love, and go into the land of Moriah, and offer him there for a burnt offering upon one of the mountains which I will tell you of.' And Abraham rose up early in the morning, and saddled his ass, and took two of his young men with him, and Isaac his son, and cut the wood for the burnt offering, and went unto the place of which God had told him.

On the third day Abraham lifted up his eyes and saw the place afar off. And he said to his young men, 'Stay here with the ass, and I and my son will go yonder and worship and come again to you.' And Abraham took the wood of the burnt offering and gave it to Isaac to carry, and he took the fire in his hand, and a knife, and they went both of them together. And Isaac spoke to Abraham his father and said, 'Behold the fire and the wood, but where is the lamb for a burnt offering?' And Abraham said, 'My son, God will provide himself a lamb.'

So they went both of them together. And they came to the place which God had told him of, and Abraham built an altar there, and laid the wood in order, and bound Isaac his son, and laid him on the altar upon the wood. And Abraham stretched forth his hand, and took the knife to slay his son. And prayed to God to put something in the way. And in the silence, like a lamb, he cut his son's throat.

2.

Without ever telling of it, because in himself he had put something in the way, Isaac succeeded in the course of years, by imagining many stories of creation and miracle for the evening and night hours, in so diverting from him his demon, whom he later called Abraham, that his demon thereupon freely performed the most wonderful and terrible exploits, which, however, lacking a preordained object, which Isaac himself was supposed to have been, did no one any harm. A free man, Isaac philosophically followed his father on his wanderings, perhaps out of a sense of responsibility, or at least forgiveness, and thus enjoyed a great and profitable entertainment to the end of his days.

HOLES

*No poem is intended for the reader, no picture for the beholder,
no symphony for the listener*

WALTER BENJAMIN

1. RESENTMENT

In the animated feature film for children, *Brother Bear*, there is a moment of the greatest profundity. Finally, after a wondrous rite of passage which involves a journey to the magical place where the lights of the aurora borealis touch the earth, three brothers embrace. But by this stage of the film they aren't ordinary brothers. As a result of their trials, one is now a spirit, one a man, and one an animal, a bear. The film thus takes us, at its moment of resolution, to the crisis of modernity. There should be no surprise that this occurs in a film for children. There is wonder in the fact that time began, but even more remarkable is the fact that it goes on. Only children sense the miracle in this – that time goes on. If we return to that moment when the three brothers embrace, three beings from the same womb now representative of three different states of being, we see in this embrace a number of possibilities: the limitation of the corporeal imagination in its conception of spirit, a limitation, it might be said, as old as imagination itself; we also see, in the distinction between man and animal, something of our own discontent, the pride of Icarus or Prometheus – that we are, indeed, more. All of this, however, though interesting, is not new. In the end the film deals not with the child's desire to be either animal or spirit – he is both already – nor with the more complex desire of the adult longing to be this child. The film, at its moment of fulfilment, because it does not know its own pathology, sings sweetly and simply of the resentment that is the very essence of the modern: that time has no end.

2. NOSTALGIA OF THE INFINITE

No event any longer comes to us without already being shot through with explanation
WALTER BENJAMIN

B. awoke from a dreamless sleep with a small hole in his left hand. The hole was not painful, apart from an occasional twinge, and when he rolled back the quilt there was no evidence of bleeding on the sheet. He scratched his chin and tried to think. He knew that if he could only think hard enough he would remember. Two black birds circled in the small sky he could see through the window from his bed. They made him shake. But he soon forgot his fear and watched with some astonishment as a thread of light passed through his open palm. On the bare wall behind the bed, the Siberian elm, which stood in the yard outside, shimmered like an intricate bonsai of itself, inverted but exact. He pulled his hand back beneath the quilt and the tree disappeared. Each morning he woke so tired it was as if the night had crushed his sleep. But he remembered nothing.

The sitting room was quiet and dark. B. could remember bricking the windows up but he could not remember why. That was the time he dismantled the ceiling lights. The empty wires, taped and stunted, pushed through the plaster like deformed joints. He had replaced the lights with small lamps which he left in the corners on the floor. The delicate lace of the lamplight spread like an incandescent fern against the ceiling. Now, as he looked at the hole in his hand, the light made him feel as if the room were closing in. He remembered the two black birds he had seen spinning in the sky. *Two workers uncovered the bones while clearing the remains of the old pavilion.* He could not remember turning the radio on.

B. often bathed with his books. He never washed himself. It was enough to feel the water cool and the skin of his stomach wrinkle. Bachofen's *Sage von Tanaquil* had been his first acquisition, and he had bought Balzac's *Peau de*

21

chagrin in 1915 at the Rümann auction put up by Emil Hirsch, but it was the rare *Fragmente aus dem Nachlass eines jungen Physikers,* which Johann Wilhelm Ritter published in two volumes at Heidelberg in 1810, that he lifted off the shelf. He liked to believe it had been a present from his father. Against his usual habit, he decided to wash the book standing up, and noticed a small hole in the instep of his right foot, like the hole in his hand, which had grown to the size of a small coin. He could see the water pass through it, but had no sensation of it doing so. He picked up a chamois from the edge of the bath and with soft strokes rubbed the book's leather covers. He was tentative at first, but as he moved to the opening pages his hand grew more assured, like a creature separate from himself. He watched the slow and gentle circle of its rub, then stopped, became aware of the radio through the door which had clicked open. His legs stiffened. For a moment he remembered the uncomfortable sensation of being watched. How often had he wished that he too were small enough to climb inside the covers of a book. And on the radio...*the bones are those of a man...*

B. cleaned his hiking boots, rubbing polish into the soft brown leather and picking at the ridged soles with a matchstick. He had a reason for cleaning the boots but had forgotten what it was. When the announcer spoke he felt the voice like clay in the tread of his boots...*who disappeared two years ago...*

— *Mr Bungle sends his regards.*

The voice came from the radio but was not the announcer's. B. dropped the boot to the floor and looked around the room.

— *There's no one else here*, the radio spoke again.

B. let his shoulders drop. He tucked his shirt into his trousers and sank in on himself, as if his head had suddenly grown so heavy he could no longer support its weight. He waited for the voice to go away.

— *You'll have to talk to me eventually*, the radio said. *I've got up the noses of harder men than you. They were a lot less clumsy, too. Why don't you try to lose some weight?*

While the radio was talking, B. edged to the corner of the room. The lamp cast his legs as a ragged arch across the ceiling. His hair fell across his face. He thought about speaking, then stopped himself.

— *Go on, fatso,* the radio goaded. *I won't bite.*

B. straightened suddenly. You're not my father, he said. He hunched back in on himself.

— The radio said, *That's better. You never know, fatso, we'll make a hero of you yet.*

Looking down at himself, B. noticed his shirt wedged strangely into his stomach.

— *That's right,* the radio said, *another one.*

B. poked his index finger gently into his stomach. It disappeared. With his other hand he reached around to his back. The hole passed through his body.

— *You're falling apart,* the radio said. *You try to make a*

virtue out of failure, with you it's always bad luck, but look at the
debris, look at the piles of debris.

B. found it increasingly difficult to move. It was as if the
air had turned to sand that he was always pushing through.
Only in front of the radio did the weight lift. The palm of
his left hand had almost disappeared and he found a new
hole that ran from the tip of his left ear down to the base
of his neck. A moth had taken up residence in the narrow
passage and its occasional fluttering was like a swooping of
birds. With his good hand he had shunted the bed into the
sitting room. He lay flat on his back in front of the radio,
the ceiling close enough to touch.

    — *Do you remember what you wrote once about Paul Klee's*
painting, Angelus Novus?

    The voice, no longer a surprise, flickered like a light,
and threw thin shadows.

    — *This is how one pictures the angel of history, you said.*
His face is turned towards the past. Where we perceive a chain of
events, he sees one single catastrophe which keeps piling wreckage
upon wreckage and hurls it in front of his feet. The angel would
like to stay, awaken the dead, and make whole what has been
smashed. But a storm is blowing from Paradise, you said, it has
got caught in his wings with such violence that the angel can no
longer close them. This storm irresistibly propels him into the future
to which his back is turned, while the pile of debris before him
grows skyward. This storm is what we call progress, you said.

    — You think I've got something to hide?

– *Listen*, the radio said, *even movement is static for you.*

– No one asked you. He was beginning to enjoy the conversation. Anyway, what makes you think I'm scared of you?

– *Look, fatso, I know you're a bit thick so I want you to listen carefully, 'cause I'll only say this once. All fear's a fear of death.*

– If only it were that simple. He thought of the holes.

– *You're thinking about failure*, the radio said. *Failure's no more than a judgement of yourself in the light of death.* B. started to speak but the radio said, *Shut up. I know what you're going to say. You think I haven't heard it before? The fear of ignorance. All right, but only if ignorance is something more than the limit death places on knowledge.*

There was a closeness in the radio's words that made him cold. He pulled the blankets over his head, burrowed in beneath the pillow.

– *No, I'll tell you, fatso, the only fear that's not a fear of death is the fear of life.*

– B.'s head poked out of the blankets. His face was stiff and shrunken. He said softly, Are you finished?

– *Against such a fear*, the radio laughed as if it had jumped on B. from behind and scared the shit out of him, *the fear of death is no more than a child's fear of the dark…*

B. had a dream. Looking down on a room. Geheime Staatspolizei, his father, mother, looking for something. He says to his father,

'What did I do?' 'This has nothing to do with you,' his father replies. 'Don't worry,' his mother says, 'we'll find it.' He starts to cry. The Gestapo say, 'Shut up.' His father kicks him in the stomach and he falls. 'Now behave,' his father says. In the far corner of the room he can see a dressing-gown cord. He crawls across the floor but although the room is small he can't reach the cord. 'What is it?' his father asks without turning. 'Nothing,' he says. They are pulling up the floorboards with a crowbar. He eases the cord out from under his mother's feet and looks for a place to hide it. He realises he is naked. 'It was him,' his father says, pointing. The Gestapo look at him and nod. An awful sound comes up through the floor. 'Can you smell it?' he says. His mother asks, 'What?' He begins to back away but there's no room to move. The Gestapo are pulling something up from beneath the floor. His father turns to them. 'Take him away,' he says. There is no mistaking the dead body on the floor. It is he.

B. realised he'd been listening to the radio.

He lived as if underground. The ceiling had dropped so low he had to work the radio off its stand and lay his mattress on the floor. He didn't mind crawling around on his hands and knees. He felt strangely light. No new holes had appeared, and the old ones had stopped growing. He rarely ate. He had no idea how his body held together. He would have liked to talk about it. Make a joke, perhaps. But he couldn't remember the last time the radio had spoken to him. He thought about his books, but the bathroom seemed too far away. He felt something like recognition, but his memory let him down, a kind of nostalgia, both sharp and pleasant, like stiffness in the joints. And the announcer's voice...*he was still alive when...*'He buried him.' He looked over his shoulder in horror as if the voice had come from outside himself. But inside, where he hoped the memory might lie uncovered, there was only blackness. When he stood, he forgot there had been a time when walking had not been possible.

B. laced his hiking boots with slow precision, careful not to twist the thin cotton ties holding the leather firm against his feet. He tucked his trouser cuffs into his socks and stood, gently brushing the creases flat and lingering over the straightness of both tongues. The door was a little stiff, but the hinges gave without a creak and light flooded in around his shoulders and feet. For a moment he had to shield his face, waiting patiently while his eyes adjusted to the brilliance. Outside, the sound of the wind. He couldn't remember digging the pit or nailing the scaffold to the Siberian elm above it. The principle was simple enough. The scaffold, heavy with soil taken from the pit, was really no more than a large trapdoor with a spring-loaded latch which could be released by pulling hard on the length of rope that hung down into the hole. B. climbed down into the pit and lay flat on his back. Two black birds circled in the small sky. He tried again to remember, then pulled hard on the rope. The latch sprang back with a click and the dirt came down swiftly in a single mass.

3. THE TASTE OF THE INVISIBLE

*There is no document of civilization which is not at the
same time a document of barbarism*

WALTER BENJAMIN

The second-hand shop on Schillstrasse is made up of two
half-shops. The proprietor, who does not like customers,
opens the shop only at those times when the street is empty.
He has spent thirty years filling the endless shelves and in
that time has not sold a single item.

In one half of the shop he sells bits of cities that he has
collected. Specks of mortar from a Parisian or Bolognese
arcade, rubble from a Roman restoration, crumbs of
masonry and concrete from towns all over Europe, and
shards of glass and tile in innumerable shapes and colours.
None of these fragments was deliberately sought, he has
no interest in destruction for himself; his pleasure comes
simply from strolling at a leisurely pace and pausing,
whenever the spirit takes him, to fill his pockets with the
debris strewn across his path. His removal of these scraps
from their natural place, their *context* as he likes to call it,
is like the breaking of tradition, and all the theft he needs.
Nothing is too small. In fact, it is his belief that one day he
will find (it might lie in his collection already, undetected),
and probably in the most unassuming fragment of rubble,
an entire city, Paris or London perhaps, built by no human
hand, but perfect and complete, just as the entire *Shema
Israel* was once inscribed on two grains of wheat.

In the other half of the shop he had started off with a collection of quotations, but after a number of years had found this collection unsatisfying. Its deliberateness disturbed him. Instead, he decided to fill the shelves with pages torn from books. He found this even more satisfying than collecting the books themselves. Once he had torn out the page he wanted, he was able to throw the book away. It was a wonderful lightness. The single page remained, like a taste of the invisible.

Although this strange existence had been forced upon the proprietor by the world into which he had been born, it is not clear whether he would not have chosen such an occupation anyway, given his temperament and his predilections. He had no desire to create, merely to find, and although he could never be thought happy, he could have gone on indefinitely in this way if not for his father. The father, of course, always wants more from his son. If he did not make a sale soon, his father had told him, he would not get another pfennig.

BREATH

The incurable imperfection in the very essence of the present moment

MARCEL PROUST

1.

I was captured the very first time I set eyes on her. She had such a marvellous way of carrying her head. The way she wore a bird of paradise in her hair. It was innate in her, and in her alone. I don't know how many times I went to the Opéra just to admire the way she walked up the staircase. I stood there and watched for her. To see her pass by with her graceful neck, and the bird looking as if it had alighted on her head of its own accord, was sheer pleasure. But apart from one or two parties to which I was invited, I didn't see much of the Comtesse. This was largely due to the jealousy of the Comte, who made no secret of the fact that he disliked me and did not wish his wife to see me. But I had my revenge, and in a way that still amuses me. It happened that Comte Greffulhe flung himself at the feet of another lady, Comtesse de La Béraudière. But she, at that time, had eyes only for me and did not know what to do to make me interested.

'What happened came much later, at a time when I was still living at Boulevard Haussmann. I would say to myself, "How could anyone with a queen like Comtesse Greffulhe at home go off to see someone like Madame de La Béraudière, who has none of her refinement, nobility or beauty?" And yet that is what he does. Apparently he is crazy about his Béraudière. Whereas for years I had been more or less fending her off, now I wanted to get to see her. Well, as you know, I was at Comtesse de La Béraudière's yesterday evening. And who else do you think was there? Comte Greffulhe! You should have seen him writhing in his chair when I was shown in. Mme. de La Béraudière could not have been more charming. And today, I visited Comtesse Greffulhe for the first time at home. I can't explain, but watching the Comte the night before, put me in mind of when I used to go to the Opéra just to see her go up the stairs. I asked her about the bird of paradise. "Oh Marcel," she said, "how can you expect after all this time...?" When I came home I took out her photograph. She used to be a beauty, and a proud woman. And to think that she will read these pages full of herself and not understand...'

2. (i)

Towards the end of the second volume of *Remembrance of Things Past*, Proust's narrator observes that his mother seems to have taken on many of his dead grandmother's traits. He concludes: 'The dead annex the living who become their replicas and successors, the continuators of their interrupted life.' We forget the dead, that is, even as our bodies become the repositories of their memories; annexed by history, our gestures repeat, perhaps eternally, what cannot be forgotten.

(ii)

The Latin word *textum* means web. No one's text is more tightly woven than Marcel Proust's; to him nothing was tight or durable enough. From his publisher Gallimard we know that Proust's proofreading habits were the despair of the typesetters. The galleys always went back covered with marginal notes, but not a single misprint had been corrected; all available space had been used for fresh text. Thus the laws of remembrance were operative even within the confines of the work. For an experienced event is finite – at any rate, confined to one sphere of experience; a remembered event is infinite, because it is only a key to everything that happened before it and after it.

– WALTER BENJAMIN, *THE IMAGE OF PROUST*

(iii)

Jean Cocteau was able to say in a beautiful essay that the intonation of Proust's voice obeyed the laws of night and honey. He recognised what really should have been the major concern of all readers of Proust and yet has served no one as the pivotal point of his reflections or his affection. Cocteau recognised Proust's blind, senseless, frenzied quest for happiness. It shone from his eyes; they were not happy but in them there lay fortune as it lies in gambling or in love.

(iv)

We do not always proclaim loudly the most important thing we have to say. Nor do we always share it privately with those closest to us, our intimate friends, those who have been most devotedly ready to receive our confession. If it is true that not only people but also ages have such a chaste – that is, such a devious and frivolous – way of communicating what is most their own to a passing acquaintance, then the nineteenth century did not reveal itself to Zola or Anatole France, but to the young Proust, the insignificant snob, the playboy and socialite who snatched in passing the most astounding confidences from a declining age as from another, bone-weary Swann. It was to be Proust's aim to design the entire inner structure of society as a physiology of chatter.

– WALTER BENJAMIN

(v)

Proust was the perfect stage director of his sickness. Even as a writer of letters he extracted the most singular effects from his malady. 'The wheezing of my breath is drowning out the sounds of my pen and of a bath which is being drawn on the floor below.' But that is not all, nor is it the fact that his sickness removed him from fashionable living. This asthma became part of his art – if indeed his art did not create it. Proust's syntax rhythmically and step by step reproduces his fear of suffocation. And his ironic, philosophical, didactic reflections invariably are the deep breath with which he shakes off the weight of memories.

(vi)

Time reveals a new and hitherto unknown kind of eternity to anyone who becomes engrossed in its passing. The eternity which Proust opens to view is convoluted time, not boundless time. His true interest is in the passage of time in its most real – that is, space-bound – form, and this passage nowhere holds sway more openly than in remembrance within and aging without. To observe the interaction of aging and remembering means to penetrate to the heart of Proust's world, to the universe of convolution. It is the world in a state of resemblances.

– WALTER BENJAMIN

(vii)

Written language begins in the trace, the magic of what remains. In this sense every word, every character in fact, is essentially ideogrammatic in its claim to stand for the thing. Even the Roman script in which these words are made carries, like memory, the scar of this trace, the echo of its magic. The words themselves are like the child's wonder of words when first he senses their connection to things and the way this connection is already a transformation, something magical: that the words in his mouth, and later, the words on the page, are connected somehow to the world beyond himself, the world beyond the page; but also that these words, when connected, become something else. In this sense a word is like a trace of what it represents – a trace, not an image.

3.

'It wasn't quite like that, but then M. Proust's stories were always a kind of rehearsal. I'll explain what actually took place in a moment. It seems like yesterday, though it's almost fifty years. It wasn't his exquisite elegance that struck me at first, but that peculiar manner, a kind of restraint, which I later noticed in many asthmatics, as though he were husbanding his breath, a gentleness more powerful than any force, an inflexible gentleness as I came to see. That was before the war, before my husband Odilon, who was his driver, received his mobilization papers, before I moved in to the apartment on Boulevard Haussmann. I didn't have the slightest sense then that I would not move out again until that moment in the rue Hamelin when he finally stopped breathing. You must forgive me if I seem too occupied with his breath. But it became my breath, too. I saw him first in a huge cloud of smoke. "Sir," I said, "you are not only a charmer, but a magician as well." The fumigations were his chief remedy against asthma, and he used always the same Legras powder. It was a dark gray powder that had to be ignited. He ordered several cartons at a time, each containing ten packets, and always from the same place – the Leclerc pharmacy in rue Vignon, at the corner of rue de Sèze. I used to buy the candles in rue Saint-Lazare. They were lighted in the kitchen, for there mustn't be the least smell of sulphur near the bedroom. Every morning – *his* morning, in other words, every afternoon – after he awoke and before he had his coffee, he "smoked". I handed him the little box; he opened it and poured the powder into the saucer, then lit it with a little square of white paper lit, in turn, from the candle. It was ordinary writing paper, which he bought at Printemps. He used to keep a box of it by the bed, carefully shut to keep out the dust. He was always afraid of dust, because of his sneezing. Sometimes he lit only a few pinches of powder, which lasted just long enough to produce some wisps of smoke. Sometimes he needed more – half an hour, an hour, several hours – then the room would be thick with smoke, as it had been the first time I entered it. His room was not only his world, it was his stage. It was when he talked to me about his childhood and youth that I began to realise he lived only in and for the dream world of his memory. The image he retained of these two periods of his life was at once affectionate and full of wonder, but without real regret or nostalgia, because to him to evoke them meant to be still living them. There was a whole way of living that he'd once known and that was crumbling gradually, in the midst of a new world coming into being...you could see his gaze looking into the past and making the comparison. "It's like a collection of beautiful antique fans on a wall," he once said to me. "You admire them, but there is no hand now to bring them alive. The very fact that they are under glass proves that the ball is over."

'Everyone who knew M. Proust was in a sense imprisoned by him and his work. It didn't bother him if people recognized themselves in his characters. In the last resort M. Proust's friendship consisted in thinking that a person deserved his analysis, which was accorded in proportion to the interest that a person represented for him, and in the end, that analysis left him with nothing but motives and explanations. All the years I knew him were one long race against time, one long pursuit of chapters and characters. He ran after time in his work, but the irony was he felt himself being overtaken. I remember once I was bold enough to ask: "Monsieur, why don't you call me Céleste? It makes me self-conscious when you call me 'madame'." And he answered: "Because, madame, I cannot." I'm sorry, I've lost the thread. What was I telling you this story for?'

4.

'If you listen closely you might still be able to hear stories of a time before the One Book. Some say there might even have been thousands of books. It is impossible, but you can hear such stories often enough to convince yourself that it might be true. Even if there were just one other, what consolation! One might speak of a world then, the word *world* might actually mean something. All words might mean something, stand for something other than themselves, for the words that were this other book, the world that was this other book. But alas, if such a journey were possible once, it is conceivable now only in dreams, or the memories of the old men who tell the stories and will soon be no more. I do not mean to sound ungrateful. I know that for centuries my ancestors laboured with a faith that defies comprehension to reach an end – you need only read, it is all there in the book. Filling all the pages first – no one has ever been able to count how many – and then, when all hope seemed lost, when no page remained yet there were still more words, devising the brilliant solution of accretion, so that every page could be added to by fixing another to its margin, and when all these too had been filled, fixing yet other pages to them, so that the book, like their memories, might expand to fill the world, the words, in the end, more real than anything that might have preceded them. I know all this for I too (like you) am an inhabitant of the book. And if there is any hope for me, if there is any dream that comes to me at night, unbiddable, like grace, it is the thought that one thing, one tiny thing, has eluded the book. Can you tell me that I am wrong?'

STONE

And if the song is sung truly,
from the whole heart, everything
at last vanishes: nothing is left
but space, the stars, the singer

OSIP MANDELSTAM

Some time in the winter of 1939, Nadezhda Mandelstam, recently widowed, made a last journey to the provincial town of Voronezh. She walked for two months on roads tanks had cleared of snow and in her dreams the sensation of walking was not unlike the roll of the sea. She walked in order to remember, inside the hexameters of her feet, each step a word that could not be committed to paper, the poems of her husband, punched like pianola rolls into the vast expanse of snow; meters measured in breaths and heartbeats. But she could not walk out these words forever; it was late and she was tired. She remembered that her husband had once said that memory was a kind of stone. He was speaking of St Petersburg. She sat down in the snow by the side of the road and slowly froze, hard as stone.

In the spring thaw the stones were not hard to find. Like her they emerged from their glass cocoons – ragstone, sarsen, chalk and flint – and as the days passed she thought of them less and less as stones. She noticed something she had not noticed for so long it made her cry. It was better if she closed her eyes. She was not a mason, nor was she a builder, but what she remembered were the puzzles her father had cut from wood and scattered on the floor for the child. One by one the odd, misshapen stones locked into place and to each she gave a word, her husband's words, the breath in the gait of her hands. It was a simple house she built, no more than a room, and she finished with the spring. A goldfinch seemed to sing to her while she built, its sharp, unpredictable turns and pitches not unlike the sound of the poems that passed through her hands in the shape of the stones: *Nadya…Nada…Nada…*It was dark where she sat. For who can build doors or windows out of stone?

The seasons vanished. She felt light now, so light it took all her concentration to keep her there; the echo of her breath more real it seemed than the breath itself. It was dark inside the room of stone and she could not see herself. No more than a voice now, as if her skin were sound, she built the house inside her head again and again, stone by stone, while her husband's words resounded all around in poems even he was yet to find.

FLAT

Without monsters and gods, art cannot enact our drama. When they were abandoned as untenable superstitions, art sank into melancholy.

MARK ROTHKO

GREEN, BLUE, GREEN ON BLUE, 1968

This painting is a story of the sea. On the deck of a savage-looking ship adorned with the bones and teeth of sperm whales, the ship's captain balances gingerly on a false leg made from a sperm whale's jaw. He announces to the crew his desire to pursue and kill the white whale who took his leg. The story of the painting lasts a long time and ends at the equator. After three days of battle with the white whale, the captain is caught in a harpoon line and snatched from the boat to his death. All of the remaining whaleboats and men, with the exception of one who floats atop a coffin, are caught in the vortex of the sinking ship and pulled under to their deaths.

NO.17/NO.15 (MULTIFORM), 1949

The painting opens with a manifesto of social thought and a meditation on domestic management, and in it the subject sketches out his ideals as he describes his project to live in the wilderness by a pond. He devotes attention to the skepticism and wonderment with which the townspeople have greeted news of his project, and he defends himself against their views that society is the only place to live. He recounts the circumstances of his move to the pond along with a detailed account of the steps he took to construct his rustic habitation and the methods by which he supported himself in the course of his wilderness experiment. In order to make a little money, he cultivates a modest bean-field, a job that tends to occupy his mornings. He reserves his afternoons and evenings for contemplation, reading, and walking about the countryside. Endorsing the values of austerity, simplicity and solitude, he consistently emphasises the minimalism of his lifestyle and the contentment to be derived from it. He contrasts his own freedom with the imprisonment of others who devote their lives to material prosperity. He makes frequent trips into town to seek the society of his long-time friends and to conduct what scattered business the season demands. On one such trip he spends a night in jail for refusing to pay a poll tax. The government, he says, supports slavery. He devotes great attention to nature, the passing of the seasons, and the creatures with whom he shares the woods. He recounts the habits of the animals, endowing them with spiritual or psychological meaning. The hooting loon that plays hide-and-seek with him becomes a symbol of the playfulness of nature and its divine laughter at human endeavours. As he becomes acquainted with the pond he decides to map its layout and measure its depth. He finds that it is no more than a hundred feet deep, refuting the common folk wisdom that it is bottomless. He meditates on the pond as a symbol of infinity that people need in their lives.

GREEN DIVIDED BY BLUE, 1968

A young boy, living in a town on the banks of a large river, discovers treasure as the result of a bold adventure, and is now kidnapped by his drunken father, who wants the gold, and imprisoned in a cabin in the wilds across the river from the town. He escapes from his father by faking his own death, killing a pig and spreading its blood all over the cabin. Hiding on an island he watches the townspeople search the river for his body and after a few days encounters a black slave who has run away from his owner after hearing her talk about selling him to a plantation down the river. The boy and the slave team up, despite the boy's uncertainty about the legality or morality of helping a runaway slave. A great storm causes the river to flood, and at one point an entire house floats past the island. The boy and the slave climb aboard to see what they can salvage, and find in it the body of a man who has been shot. The slave refuses to let the boy see the dead man's face. They capture a raft and have a series of adventures: a close encounter with a gang of robbers on a wrecked steamboat; the separation of the pair after another steamboat slams into their raft; the boy's participation in a bloody feud between two aristocratic families; and a sequence of scams carried out by two confidence men whom the pair encounter after the slave rescues the boy on the repaired raft. In the end, the confidence men sell the slave to a farmer. The boy resolves to free him and to his surprise is mistaken for a good friend he has left behind in his home town. The people now holding the slave are his friend's aunt and uncle. When his friend turns up at the farm, a new series of adventures ensues amongst all the confusion of mistaken and assumed identities, culminating in the freeing of the slave (who has been a free man all along), and the revelation that the dead man discovered in the floating house had been the boy's father. The boy, who by this time has had enough of civilization, rejects the offer of his friend's aunt to adopt him, and resolves to set out for the West.

GETHSEMANE, 1944

the beginning & the end first & last family saga brothers obsession with a sister 4 voices 4 days deterioration of a culture all there in one the first the gelded idiot hes 33 its easter through the fence between the curling flower spaces he watches a game of golf & remembers his sister mostly hes 3 & hes with his 2 brothers & their grandmother has died though they dont know it & his sister is the only one brave enough to climb the pear tree & look through the window

at the funeral wake while her brothers stand below gazing
up at her muddy drawers & he remembers her perfume in
1905 & her lost virginity in 1909 & her wedding in 1910
& his own change of name his brother the mausoleum of
all hope & desire who drowned himself in 1910 puts 2 flat
irons in his pockets because nothing remains of his familys
noble & glorious past except his sisters loss of honour & the
daughter born to her to whom she also gave his name &
the idiot remembers all this & other things too the events
at the gate in 1910 & his father dead & the broken flower
drooping over his fist as he begins to howl

THE BLACK AND THE WHITE, 1956

I came from the Midwest to New York in the summer of
1922 to learn about the bond business. I rented a house
on Long Island. Not long after moving in I had dinner
with my cousin and discovered that her husband, whom
I'd known at Yale, was having an affair with a woman who
lived in a valley of ash, a gray industrial dumping ground
between my home and the city. Not long after this I met
my neighbour at one of his Saturday night parties. He told
me he had met my cousin in 1917 and was still deeply
in love with her, that he spent most nights staring at the
green light at the end of her dock across the bay from his
mansion. He wanted me to arrange a reunion. Eventually,
I learnt the true story of his past. He was born in North
Dakota and changed his name when he was seventeen.
A gold baron served as his mentor, and though he inherited

nothing of the man's fortune on his death, it was he who first introduced my neighbour to the world of wealth and privilege. You might say he invented himself then. But my cousin's husband was growing increasingly suspicious of his wife's relationship and in a suite at the Plaza Hotel he announced to my cousin that my neighbour was a criminal. She realised her allegiance then, you might say, and he sent her back home with my neighbour, signalling to all how little he had to fear. If it wasn't ugly then, it quickly became so. While driving home she accidentally hit and killed her husband's mistress. My neighbour, unable to see that his dream now would never be realised, took the blame and was himself killed by the woman's husband, shot and left to die in his own swimming pool. I moved back West after that. Strangely, I think I fell in love with him in the same way he fell in love with my cousin, with the idea of him at any rate. But everywhere you looked it was empty – the era of dreaming was over.

BLUES

All music is folk music

BOB DYLAN

IT TAKES A LOT TO LAUGH,
IT TAKES A TRAIN TO CRY

I am not by nature a suspicious man. The stranger has no need to lie, and even if he did, I have no need to disbelieve. 'While you were here washing glasses,' the stranger might say, his papery face in need of a shave, 'I was there when it happened.' Truth also has its borders, its poles of ice, and natives tall as trees. The storytellers know that I never leave the mountains. That the fire here costs no more than a tale. What use have I for gold? There are broad beans here, wild herbs that grow beneath the almond trees by the stream, and pigeons that I snare when meat is a need. I cannot read. The traveller who left these pages had a dreamy desolate face. He no longer had a tongue. He filled the few scraps of paper that I had and would not eat or sleep. The lines of ink are small and close.

Perhaps, one morning out of the snow, someone will emerge with time to read a story to an ignorant old man.

MOTORPSYCHO NITEMARE
'Yes, I saw him once,' the foreigner says, looking up from the smallest of the pages. 'It must have been four years ago. The time of the crowds.'

Nov. 1. The safety pin through the nose was a nice touch. She wore identical silver pins in each earlobe. Her head was shaved to a stubble and tattooed with jasmine flowers that tailed down her neck and disappeared beneath the collar of a black bomber jacket whose sleeves had been cut off at the shoulders. Her jeans, too, had been cut off, and there were tears in the back which had not been patched. Her legs were pale, milky almost like pearl, and vanished just above the knees into black jackboots whose lace holes were clamped together with painted safety pins. Her eyes were glazed and she moved towards me with a narcotic silkiness. The hunting knife hung from a thin strap around her left thigh. (It did not glint in the sun. I thanked God.)

Jan. 5. When the rains didn't come, I watched the weeds grow out of the stone and ate them before they flowered. I couldn't keep (them) down.

Feb. 7. I slept on the rock. (It was five years before I built the pallet.)

Mar. 23. I know what you're thinking, Anthony lay down with the lion and Jeremy said Help me God and the whole company of demons disappeared. I waited ten years to be noticed, for Christ's sake.

May 16. The snakes are real, so are the rats, the thieves who won't believe I've got nothing to hide. Everything is real. Bastard!

Aug. 12. ...I filled the pallet with brambles and thorns and dry cut-grass...

Aug. 13. Heaven hates what it hates. (I repeat: HEAVEN HATES WHAT IT HATES.)

Oct. 30. A technique for penitence – it takes one thorn – you line it up with the base of your spine and push yourself back and forth against the pallet frame – if the thorn is strong enough it'll reach the bone – there's no chance you won't black out.

Nov. 1. I can remember what they wrote, that I really was never any more than what I was – a folk musician who gazed into the grey mist with tear-blinded eyes and made up songs that floated in a luminous haze. When would I realise I wasn't a prophet performing miracles?

Nov. 31. Somewhere in the cave she removed her jacket and boots. (In the shadows, the monk with the bowl of apricots, the nicks on his scalp were still fresh. I should have noticed. Is one vision too much to ask?)

Her breasts were small and tattooed. There was a safety pin
through each nipple. I cried out Help me Father.
(Her calves were smooth and brushed against my legs.)
She slipped the knife out of the strap.
The Lord is my helper, I will not fear.
I closed my eyes, but she wouldn't go, she wouldn't go away. I saw
it, like all the rest, God, like all the rest, I saw it, she was real like
all the rest…The line of blood where the knife had cut her hip.
(…the glint of light against glass…of cameras…)

Dec. 25.

I DREAMED I SAW ST AUGUSTINE

The foreigner stops and dips his bread into the thick gravy
on his plate. He has eaten everything, even the scraggy feet.
I've seen it often enough, not the hunger, but the look, as
if they're going back to the place. When the bread is gone
he will talk.

'I do little business in the desert,' he says, wiping his
mouth with a large handkerchief. He is gaunt but clean.
Few men have time to wash who cross the mountains.
Those that do have something to sell. He says, 'Times
aren't what they were.' He looks at me and I nod. I look
at the snow outside the window and am reminded of what
another traveller once told me about the city, desolate with
rubbish as anonymous as the drifting junk of the sea, noises
animal and close, wild mongrel dreams, random yelps that
punctuated the night like falling stars.

'The desert's a quiet place,' he says, 'grey, colourless, kind of. But this day the whole plain's covered in tents and trucks, there's people everywhere, even a helicopter, low enough to be throwing up a lot of dust...' I fill his glass. The red markings on his face could be from the sun. I can feel his feet beneath the table as he shifts in his chair. He continues speaking, though more slowly, as if he is waiting for it all to happen. He doesn't thank me for the drink. 'A woman told me she'd come because she'd heard he could heal. Said he'd gone out there to hear the voice of the universe, that the music of the spheres was pure folk. I never saw him or the cave...' I nod again. I can feel the end. The traveller, too, is quiet for some time, and looks at me in an odd way, like he can see beyond the moment. When he speaks his voice is dry, the words parched and brittle. 'There were cameras everywhere, and the sun...the heat, and the sharpness of everything...but it wasn't only the heat, I can't explain it, it was in me, I was shivering and there was this...' I can feel his shaking through the table. His face has lost its colour. Even if I could speak, I would not contradict the stranger's story. 'I heard his voice,' he says, his own voice as the snow against the window. His eyes are on me but he doesn't see. I know that look too. 'I was running through the crowd but I knew it was him. They were calling him Saint. He said: "In a few years time a shit storm will be released. Things will begin to burn. The road out will be treacherous. You won't know where it leads, but follow it anyway. It is a strange world ahead that will unfold. A thunderhead of a world with jagged lightning edges. Many will get it wrong and never get it right. Some will go straight into it. It's wide open. One thing is for sure, not only is it not run by God, it isn't run by the devil either." That's what he said. I didn't think I'd remembered.'

The stranger's head falls forward onto the table. I fold his coat and push it under his forehead. Some men are still pursued by sleep.

TEMPORARY LIKE ACHILLES

The traveller's words did not surprise me. I had heard the same, it must have been three years before. Or perhaps earlier. There was a time, before the storms, when the television transmitters could still reach the mountains. I heard the voice on a news program late at night. Outside, the rusted cries of owls, and their swoop. It was still the time of the seasons, spring, and there were wood mice everywhere. And limes. This really happened, the voice said. I knew enough then to know you can do anything with a camera.

Scene i
The mouth of a small cave.
Three men with stiff beards and frizzled hair are chanting. One man's body is covered in a golden flame which crackles without burning. Another hovers in a kneeling position, a foot off the ground. The last pours red wine from a crude clay jug onto the dirt. Inside the cave a shadow with glowing eyes peers out from behind the rock.

Scene ii
NEWSREADER:...no one knows the exact time of his arrival.
There are those who claim they have witnessed his struggles with
the devil, convinced the attacks are real, more cross the mountains
every day, but his motives remain a mystery and he will not
speak...

Scene iii
Inside the cave.
A man all head and bone writhes on a wooden pallet. On the
walls, dancers' slender hands flicker. There is no sound. A fat
man in a grey business suit, with greased hair and thin waxed
moustaches, sits in a corner throwing black grapes at dogs whose
long teeth are purple with the juice. He has a thin but fixed smile.
Through the glassy floor of the cave the desert can be seen as if in a
photograph taken from a height. The ground rushes away.

I used to get excited by television. This really happened,
the voice said. You can see my problem. I suppose they
thought we didn't really care any more about the difference. The strange thing is, though, even if it were true, it
wouldn't be any more special.

GIRL FROM THE NORTH COUNTRY

There was a village here before the storms. The foreigners
look doubtful when I show them the photographs. A man
who lives alone needs a good memory, but even more, he
needs to believe that what he remembers is true. I showed

the technician who came to look at the television a photograph of my wife. There was nothing wrong with the television. He said the problem was the signals.

I gave him a drink and he told me about his brother. He said it was my wife made him think. I would have liked to ask him if it was that he saw her as I once did, the new moon faint in the twilight and her moth eyebrows quivering. His brother disappeared. They thought he was dead. Then they got a letter. A traveller brought it out of the desert. It seems the brother picked up a hitchhiker who told him about some hermit who lived in the desert. She had a small piece of his tongue which she carried in a handkerchief and would not let him see. She was tubercular and dying. They drove for over a week and only stopped to...The technician said his brother was always a sucker for a pretty face and a tall story. I nodded. He pulled a page out of his pocket and unfolded it carefully. It had that powdery quality paper gets when it's handled a lot. He read: 'Brother, you wouldn't believe if I told you, there are priests here, and doctors and painters and women with flowers in their hair, good people. They live outside the cave and sleep beneath the stars, in peace, his voice, he heals people with his words, they've written them down somewhere, *I crave visions,* that's one I heard, *and you send me girls with safety pins.* He doesn't believe in his own miracles. It's wonderful, he thinks the TV companies set them up. *You've got to have power and dominion over the spirits,* he'll say. *I had it once and once was enough. Someone'll come along eventually who'll have it again, someone* who can see into things, the truth of things, not metaphorically, but really, like seeing into metal and making it melt, see it for what it is and reveal it for what it is with hard words and vicious insight. Come, if you really want to be with me you'll find the way.' He laughed like a man does when he knows he's got nothing left. He patted me on the shoulder when he went. Told me that some people seem to fade away but when they're truly gone, it's like they didn't fade away at all.

    I try, of a night, to get the television to work.

BALLAD OF A THIN MAN

Some men are still pursued by sleep. And I...

A moth-eyed woman with a tattooed back undresses carefully in front of a large mirror. Behind her, a man sits on the edge of a bed. He looks through a window at a small van vibrating on the edge of the road, its exhaust fumes like a lens. He looks through them to the lime trees, giant and shimmering. Then back to the woman who is tying her hair in a knot behind her head. Occasionally, holding her stockings in her hand, she will turn and speak urgently to him, but he will not reply. He can't stop looking at the giant limes. The woman rises reluctantly and walks to the door of the room. He hears her voice again. He watches as she climbs into the passenger side of the van, which drives off, the lime trees shrinking as the fumes seep into the air. Only then does he become aware of a fat man in a grey business suit, with greased hair and thin waxed moustaches. He knows who it is. The fat man hands him a knife. Slowly, he pushes his mouth over the blade. The fat man smiles thinly.

BOOTS OF SPANISH LEATHER

If a man could pass through Paradise in a dream, & have a flower presented to him as a pledge that his soul had really been there, & if he found that flower in his hand when he awoke – Aye, & what then?

BOXES

1.

In December 1946, Joseph Cornell, who had long been an expert collector, became something of a curator. He had not planned the theft. The theatre was on Third Avenue. The movie was William Dieterle's *Love Letters*; its star, the tender and wistful Jennifer Jones. In the dark he watched her through the closed fingers of both hands. He hid, when the lights came up, behind a black curtain that hung beside the projection booth. He watched the credits roll. The screen blazed for a moment; then it too went black. The projectionist had already lit a cigarette, the smoke trailing him in wisps as he walked out. Cornell slipped into the vacant booth and worked quietly, unrolling the film in forearm lengths. He found the scene he wanted and cut off ten frames, stolen lovingly, he thought, like a lock of hair, or a single glove. He is in the booth still.*

1.

In December 1946, Joseph Cornell, who had long been an expert collector, became something of a curator. He was following a girl who looked like Jennifer Jones. He liked to think of them as butterflies, the girls crossing Roosevelt and Main in autumn sunlight. The girl who looked like Jennifer Jones went into Woolworths and wandered all over the store, daydream shopping. He remembered then that he was wearing a sandwich board, not stencilled with advertisements for restaurants or the movies like the professional 'sandwich men', but covered with rescued objects that were glued or nailed to the boards, one object overlapping the next: ticket stubs, cigar and candy wrappers, keys, metal gears, the tap from a shoe bottom, yellow leaves, a busted fob watch, a woollen sock. The girl who looked like Jennifer Jones did not turn her head as he followed her home.*

1.

In December 1946, Joseph Cornell, who had long been an expert collector, became something of a curator. His studio, the basement of 3708 Utopia Parkway, Flushing, New York, was not constructed of bricks and mortar, but grew like a pearl from the secretions of his pockets. Beneath whatever was happening in the rooms above, the walls and passages grew shelves filled with boxes, their handwritten labels like traces, clues: best white boxes Empty, watch parts, plastic shells, wooden balls, Glasses, Dürer, Tinfoil, Caravaggio etc., Cordials, magazine and newspaper articles, photographs, costume trimmings, glass ice cubes, miscellaneous, Love Letters/Jennifer Jones.*

Notes

* In the Art Institute of Chicago is a box entitled *Untitled (Butterfly Habitat)*. The box is divided into six windows; through each we see a butterfly. Cornell splattered the windows with white paint, creating the illusion of a layer of frost or snow. In the middle of each window he cleared away a circular aperture like a child might make using a glove, allowing the viewer to see each butterfly. The box is old and worn; the wooden mullions dividing it into separate compartments, brittle and cracked. The condition of the box contrasts with the pristine state of the butterflies, magically preserved. The catalogue entry reads: 'This compulsion to box and encase can be seen as a form of necrophilia, a tendency to transform objects into dead possessions. Cornell *kills* in order to love.'

DISQUIET

How difficult to be just oneself and not see anything but the visible

FERNANDO PESSOA

There is in Lisbon an eminent writer, Alberto Caeiro, who has been awarded many decorations in his lifetime; indeed, he possesses so many Portuguese and foreign orders that, whenever he has to put them all on, his critics call him 'the iconostasis'. He moves in the most distinguished circles – at least during the last twenty-five or thirty years there has not been a single famous scholar or writer in Europe with whom he has not been intimately acquainted. He is an honorary Fellow of all the Portuguese and three foreign universities. Etcetera, etcetera.

All this, and a great deal more, makes up what is known as my name. This name of mine is well known. It is known to every educated person in Europe, it is mentioned by university lecturers with the addition of the adjectives 'celebrated' and 'esteemed'. It is among those few fortunate names which it is considered bad taste to abuse or speak of disrespectfully in public or in print. And so it should be. For my name is closely associated with the idea of a man who is famous, richly endowed, and most certainly useful. I am as hard-working and as hardy as a camel, which is important, and I am talented, which is even more important. Besides, I may as well add that I am a well brought up, modest, and honest fellow. I have never poked my nose into politics, never sought popularity by engaging in polemics with ignoramuses, and never made speeches at dinners or at the graves of my colleagues…There is in fact not a single blot on my name as a writer, and I have no complaints to make.

My name is as brilliant and attractive as I myself am dull and unprepossessing. My head and hands tremble from weakness; my chest is hollow and my back narrow. There is nothing impressive in my wretched figure; it is only perhaps when I suffer from the tic that I get a peculiar expression which in anyone who happens to look at me at the time provokes the stern and impressive thought: 'That man will probably die soon.' Which is why I must set the record straight. For a certain man has put it about that I do not exist. Or to put it more accurately, that I am no more than my name, which in itself is a creature of his invention. That I am no more than the autobiography of a man who never existed. I'll let you be the judge of that. Let me tell you a story.

Early in life, when he had not yet become a writer, in the barren hills beyond Lisbon, Fernando António Nogueira Pessoa became, for a time, the keeper of sheep. And every evening, as the sun dropped behind the hills, he would lead his flock back to the small corral where he kept them overnight. He would stand at the open gate and hold a stick across the entrance, horizontal to the ground, so that the sheep had to jump over it in order to pass into the yard. He had no idea why he did this, could not remember when he started this strange practice, but it delighted him to watch, as one by one the sheep jumped over the stick and into the corral. One evening, overcome, perhaps, by a small demon, he held the stick in place as he did on every other evening, but then, after the first sheep had jumped over it, he pulled the stick away. What he saw this time, however, gave him no delight. He watched as one by one the remaining sheep jumped over the stick that wasn't there and trotted off into the yard. He repeated this again the following evening, and the evening after that. There was no stick, and yet the sheep continued to jump as if there were. And for some reason their jumping filled him now with an unnameable dread.

BONES

sometimes we feel we're about
to uncover an error in nature

EUGENIO MONTALE

Eugenio Montale's mother had eyes like the undersides of mushrooms. 'You have to crawl before you can walk,' she had told him as a boy, 'but no matter how much walking you do you'll never fly.' He would have liked to believe her. He liked to think of himself as a man of reason. But this morning he'd seen something which he couldn't explain. While he was walking by the sea he heard what he thought was the voice of a young woman. When he looked up, the only thing he could see was a small black bird. He knew that a bird could not talk, but what was even stranger was that he too began to fly. And below him, the sand turned the colour of the sky.

In his later years he preferred to live alone. He slept in

the day and rose only after dark. Sometimes he went for a walk at night and the Milanese streets were so quiet he imagined a world without sound. On these nights he talked to himself. 'I will leave the city,' he said, 'and build a boat and live forever on the sea.' But he never built a boat. Evenings when he woke, the sea filled his ears like the inside of a shell.

In the Villa Vieusseux he sat, waiting for the miracle. 'You can't chase two rabbits,' the lemon tree said. Everything singing. Rocks rubbed smooth by the sea: 'What is beauty but a moment that will not pass?' The acanthus that no one knew: 'This morning when you cut my hair I thought of nothing but the moment of your breasts against my still arm.' Eel limpid in the half-dried pool: 'Sometimes I dream I am a snail and the slow world is as beautiful as a Greek vase.' Then silence, the brittle bones of the stars: 'And poetry imitates death.' That evening, when he left the woman's bed, even the fisherman folding the mist in his net did not turn his head.

He wasn't always comfortable in open spaces. There was a time the wind disturbed him. He couldn't be certain if it was the sound, or the way it felt against his skin. He would wear trousers, a long cotton shirt, and a scarf wrapped around his ears and face. He would walk with his hands in his pockets. When the young men walked past with their girls on their arms he would smile. They would not see the night. There was a time he could have told them every colour of the sea. Now his mind was on other things. The way a coffee drop would draw out the grain of a page like a fingerprint. He had almost worked out how to space the cups. Soon he would never have to sleep.

BLINDNESS

1.

I n the beginning, when I told people what I did for a living, they'd look at me as if I'd just returned from the grave.

I've heard it said that a man without secrets is no one — powerless; nothing hidden, nothing left, I've heard say.

Towards the end, my wife found a phrase, she might even have made it up, it doesn't matter. 'They mightn't be the facts,' she'd say, 'but it's the truth.'

He wasn't sure when it began, the morning his wife left him most likely, he attributed a lot to that morning, his drinking, for instance, and the nights of fitful somnambulance, he began to think *of it as a kind of year zero, the morning the world was created, the morning he photographed his first ghost.*

I think I can say with some accuracy that I am not a perverse man. I was married for twenty years. But when my wife left me, I developed an interest in paintings. Yesterday I discovered the technique for photographing ghosts while watching a small landscape that used to hang above the dining table...

Mrs—— stopped reading and laid the page face down on the table. Borges could tell she wasn't happy. Why should she be? A whole day, and all he could come up with was a photographer who talked like a used-car salesman with a penchant for paintings.

'I'll leave you to it then, shall I?' Mrs—— finally said, considering a small plate of iced cakes as if there had been no silence. Although his host's capacity to inhabit a world of seamless time disturbed the writer, he spoke calmly, as if he too knew the secret. 'Please, don't leave on my account.'

It was almost a month now since Borges had read the small advertisement in *La Nación*. The freedom it promised had made him blush, but even more inexplicable to him was the kind of woman who would make such a promise. A large, self-contained suite of rooms in her own house, and everything the writer might need. His only obligation – to read each night at dinner what he had written during the day. But now he couldn't even do that; he would rather work fifteen hours a day in a factory than do that. In the one month he had been there, she had not made a single comment on his work.

'I know writers,' Mrs—— spoke again, continuing the conversation. 'Your time is far too precious.' Borges was about to speak, he heard her words as clues to something hidden, but the woman had risen from the table and walked so languidly to the door it was as if time had stopped, as if he had become a snail, and the slow world as beautiful as a Greek vase. He was still looking at her long after she had left the room.

Borges had no idea if Mrs—— was as beautiful as he thought, and he knew of no test. She was a woman, yes, but she seemed to have no sense of herself as a woman; no sense, that is, of his gaze. She sat at the table, dressed in frilled underpants and a brassiere, yet she behaved with such naturalness and unselfconsciousness, and moved so gracefully, it wasn't until after she left the room that he became aware that he had been sitting across the table from an almost-naked woman. It was like waking from an enchantment. Her sublime indifference to the effect her body had on him made her gestures as unreadable as a hieroglyph. She seemed exquisitely artless – if not for her mask. Borges had never seen her face. But at night, when he tried to forget, it wasn't the smooth skin of her thighs, the fleshy stomach or small breasts, it wasn't even the dark birthmark visible beneath the pale red hair on the back of her neck – no, he could not sleep because her mask would not let him sleep. It was a man's face, he was certain of that, and so perfect in its detail it had to be funerary, modelled over the features of the corpse, and cast in gold. It was the finest mask he had ever seen. But no matter how closely he looked, or from what angle, he could not determine where the mask ended and her skin began. And she behaved not only as if the mask were not there, but as if only a fool would think otherwise. Mrs—— had no age. And of a night, when he slept, he saw not what her face might be, but that delicate man's face, depthless and without body, whirling through the darkness of his room, dancing to the tune of a Chopin waltz.

2.

No one knew of Mrs——'s diary. Whenever she felt like writing she would lock herself in her bedroom and remove the worn red vellum album from the middle drawer of her small French kneehole desk. The key, inlaid with the same pictorial marquetry as the desk, never left her. This evening it was attached to a thin gold necklace. Her plan was beautifully simple. With dates set ten years into the past, she would record the details of Borges' life, as if he were her husband. Mrs—— wrote for the future, for some unknown eyes which, long after her death, would see that she did indeed have a past, and that her life, like every other, had a beginning and an end.

She wrote now, on an old Olivetti, assuming Borges' voice.

DECEMBER 15, 1945   *9.40 P.M.*
If there is one axiom I hold above all others, it is that characters

cannot be created from imagination. Writing from imagination is like composing a photograph but neglecting to load the camera with film. No, the only way to write is to steal. The true writer can have no sacred cows. I love my wife, but that's all the more reason not to spare her. It's not a question of morality. If I could, I'd tell her. But then she'd realise I was only betraying her for my work, and her responses wouldn't be real. And real responses are what readers want. No, it's got nothing to do with ethics. I'm talking about the truth. And even if I wasn't, it hurts me too. Is guilt any less poignant than betrayal? If someone were to ask me why I got interested in the story of a man who withheld sexual favours from his wife, I couldn't say. I just did. And if I can keep it up, God knows what riches will emerge. She won't say anything, but I can feel it. I can smell it. Two days ago I heard her in the kitchen, whispering to a woman. The woman was examining her palm.

'It's not hopeless,' she said. 'But it won't be easy.'

My wife began to unbutton her blouse.

'No,' the woman barked. She reached down to a basket by her feet. My wife said something I couldn't hear, and the woman handed her a small wooden pillbox.

Marvellous. That's what I mean. Does anyone truly believe they can conceive something like that out of nothing?

'The art of the erotic is not revelation,' I heard the woman say as she was leaving. Her face was sharp, like a bird's, and her crimson skirt billowed like a silken concertina. 'No, the art of the erotic is concealment, the gradual process of concealment.'

Mrs—— thought of the advertisement she had placed

almost a month ago and smiled. She was not at all unhappy
with the result. She went over the writer's features once again
in her mind. As with the advertisement she had placed ten
years before, and the two in between, her heart quickened at
the lure. Nothing in this world awakened her to life so much
as the furtive moment of seduction – and unfinished love.

3.

In his calmer moments, Borges believed he was going mad.
Not a madness that made him want to dance naked in the
rain, but a wasting, febrile, luscious madness. Whatever
he touched, he touched Mrs——; wherever he looked, he
saw the mask of her face. It was as if the world had become
a vast and voluptuous paramour whose desire was for him
alone. And there was no escape. When he closed his eyes
and sat perfectly still, the air was like a caress from that
almost-naked body. He felt he would die. The solution
was self-evident: simply tell her of his love. But he knew
that such a confession would appear to her as brutal as an
explosion. She wanted a writer. He had seen the way her
hand fluttered above the table in the silence after reading,
the threads of moisture on her neck and the fine quiver in
the lace of her brassiere, he had seen the same telltale signs
almost every night. The first story had been a failure, but in
that impossible opening which he had handed to her what
seemed a lifetime ago, he had dared to hope. What a fool he
had been! The voice, the character, the point of view, were
so wrong as to be almost laughable. What could he have

been thinking? It was only the delicacy of her sensibility that prevented her from throwing him out on his ear there and then. Mrs—— wanted a story. If he could not write of his love in such a way that she would find it irresistible, if he could not entice her to see the story as in some way allegorical, he might as well dance naked in the rain. And so Borges found it almost impossible to write, even as he saw writing as his only hope of salvation.

If someone had taken him aside and told him gently that it was a dream, he would have believed them, so unbelievable was the success of his first collection of ghosts. His own particular favourite was the photograph of Sir Arthur Conan Doyle, whom he had never seen, but the crowds were flocking to the photograph of Columbus, and the newspapers were full of his image of Christ, which he had discovered inadvertently, while taking dawn shots of the slagheaps at the edge of the city. He learnt early that ghosts inhabited unexpected places, and although most of his real treasures came from paintings, he had developed the habit of photographing everything he saw. Of course, there were those who doubted the integrity of the enterprise and described the exhibition as a sham, but even if, as the doubters claimed, there were no portraits of Christ that might be used as tests, there could be no mistaking the reality of the stigmata on Christ's hands, through which his body could be seen, nor the awe which every day drew more and more people to the gallery. The ghosts resembled living people (if anything, they were even more substantial), but the photographs were strange in that the figures seemed to emerge from the negative, the entire background remained negative, as if, paradoxically, the final

~~print retained both its developed and undeveloped state. The secret of his discovery was that, because the camera could photograph ghosts, it was unable to photograph anything real or living.~~

Borges paused for a moment and looked up at the painting on the wall opposite his desk. A Chinese landscape, pale green and muddy rice fields beneath an overcast sky. It made him shudder. Figures in the painting, tiny figures, so tiny he hadn't noticed them, out against the horizon of mist, picking rice. The story about the photographer was rubbish. Where was the fear? He thought the woman would like the softer third-person voice, but he needed to bring it back to something human, dramatic – something that spoke plainly, though elusively, of love.

~~The photographer remembered one of his wife's more prophetic comments. 'You're so bad,' she said, 'you'd get jealous of me looking at a fucking painting.'~~

Borges didn't like the phrasing; it felt clumsy and brutal. He was reading everything with the woman's eyes. What did he want her to feel? For a moment he thought of changing it. For a moment he wanted only to punish – himself? Her? He continued to write, submitting finally to the erection whose possibility he had been aware of for some time. He thought of Mrs——, how she might respond to the love between a man and a painting, and wondered what kind of painting she would be.

It didn't happen immediately, around the time he had taken the roll of film that hadn't developed – he began to feel as if he were being watched. For a time the feeling disturbed him, and he moved uneasily around the house, but it didn't take long before he began to enjoy the sensation. Of a night he would undress with his back to the paintings; everything he did became charged by this invisible gaze. One night, waking from a half-sleep on his couch, he caught sight of the small landscape. He stood up and closed all the windows and curtains, then walked across to the painting and stared at the floor while he stroked the smooth edges of the frame. He lifted it gently from the wall and held it against his chest, no longer conscious of the blindness he was opening up inside himself. That night, he discovered he already knew the secret of photographing ghosts.

For some reason, he thought of the advertisement in *La Nación*. A single sentence, buried in the sober and mathematical detail of what anyone, surely, must have regarded as a strange proposal.

Due to the influence of my late husband, a writer of no small esteem, I am fortunately (or unfortunately, I cannot be certain) unable to feel directly.

And the late afternoon he walked nervously through the sculptured gardens and held his breath as he let the heavy knocker fall against the door of the enormous house. 'I'm a writer,' he said, when the door opened and a figure stood hidden in the shadow. 'I haven't written anything in a long time.'

He had had no intention of making the last confession, but something in the figure's silence had drawn it out. 'You'll write here,' was all the figure said. It might have been that he was standing outside in the twilight, but as his eyes adjusted to the shadow he felt a terrible vertigo. Somehow he was looking, not at the figure, but through it to the room beyond. And even as the moment passed, and the figure became a woman in a nightgown of black lace, beckoning him to enter, he could not see her face...

One morning, while walking through the park close to his home, he was approached by two men. Before he had time to realise what was happening, one of the men ripped the camera off his shoulder and photographed him with it, while the other, with a camera of his own, photographed the act. The first man then handed back his camera and said: 'Thank you.' His partner said: 'We needed a picture for the story we're running.' The men spoke quietly and politely. As they walked away, the photographer looked down at his camera. He had never thought of photographing himself.

In the quiet afterglow of memory, drained of all desire but vaguely conscious of a new possibility, Borges gave himself up to sleep.

4.

'Mrs——, when I was still a young man, I formed for myself an ideal of the woman I should love. It seems my whole life has gone by, and now, for the first time, I have met what I thought – in you. I love you and offer you my hand.'

Borges, rehearsing his proposal, stopped suddenly at the dining room door. Mrs——, bent over the table, was wrapped in the most beautiful sari he had ever seen, her hands rearranging flowers in a white vase while she spoke to a shadow that stopped in the garden outside the frosted window.

'There are two things I love,' she called in her shy, breathless voice. 'The smell of chrysanthemums after rain.'

She did not straighten or turn when she heard Borges approaching, but her sudden stillness told him that she felt his presence and was excited by it.

'Well, Mr Borges, how was your writing?' she asked, turning her masked face to him and gently extending her hand from a loose fold of red silk.

'I can no longer tell,' he said, staring at her small bare feet while he placed the wrinkled pages in her hand. For a moment their fingers touched. 'Please,' he said.

Mrs—— did not answer. She sat at the table and began to read. 'Help yourself to a drink,' she said, pointing to a narrow lacquered cabinet without lifting her head. Apart from the table, the cabinet was the only piece of furniture in the room that was not covered by a dustsheet. Borges did not move immediately, and when he did he walked backwards, slowly, keeping his eyes on the woman, who seemed to tremble as she read. Before he reached the cabinet, Mrs—— stood up. Borges had never seen her in daylight, and was struck once again by the way she appeared to grow more substantial as the night progressed. He listened as the soft silk brushed against her skin.

'What are you going to call your story?' she asked.

'It doesn't have a title.'

They walked a few steps in silence. Mrs—— saw that he wanted to speak; she divined what it was that he wished to say, and trembled slightly with anticipation. She saw it in his glasslike hair, his pale, watchful face, narrow and deep-lined. She saw it in his hesitant stoop, the wary stillness of his tall frame and the meditative curve of his hands; she saw his desolation and grew faint. They walked twice around the room, but still he did not speak. She would have been better to remain silent. Hadn't she worked the whole thing out in advance? She knew it would be easier for him to say what he wanted to say after a silence. But against her will, as if by accident, Mrs—— said: 'Why doesn't the photographer have a name?'

Borges sighed and made no answer. Why, after weeks of silence, had she chosen this moment to talk about his writing? His mind whirled. If only he could guess what she wanted. He felt, as surely as he felt the body brushing against his own, that he was close. But his skin was burning, and against his own will, instead of talking about the story, about how from the very first word he had conceived it as an allegory of his love for her, he looked at the delicate cloth cupped at her breasts and spoke about saris.

'Once there was a sari maker who spun the most

beautiful silk in all Kashmir,' he said. 'One day he was summoned by the Empress and commanded to make seven saris, one for each colour of the rainbow. He worked for five years on the spinning, dyeing and weaving of the silk. Expecting great reward for his labour, he brought the completed saris to the Empress, who was overcome by their beauty. When finally she was able to take her eyes off his creations, she ordered that the sari maker's hands be cut off.'

A few more minutes passed. Mrs—— continued walking, conscious of nothing but the man who had dropped one step behind her. She had come close, yet somehow she had failed. She knew now that he desired her, but something in her manner or her dress had been too brutal. A man like Borges, so ethereal, could only be won by the greatest subtlety. The slightest threat to his writing would drive him away. But what could she do? She was at the limit of her imagination. She had followed her art to the finest detail, and when the moment had come, he had told a story about clothes. Never before had she felt so strongly the need to speak the truth (never before had she failed), but she couldn't guess the writer's mind, and now in a moment her fate was to be decided. She was mortally afraid – afraid of both his speaking and not speaking.

Now or never was the moment for his declaration. Borges felt that everything about Mrs—— – the reproachful turn of the head, her agitated step, and the fine lines of sweat across her wrist and neck – betrayed painful suspense. Even the gold cheeks of her mask seemed slightly burnished, as if flushed by an internal heat. He felt sorry for her. He even felt that to keep silent now would be to wrong her. He thought again of the way she appeared in his sleep, how he had tried to believe that it wasn't really his writing that she wanted, that no woman could advertise blatantly for love. He even repeated to himself the words in which he had intended to put his offer, but over these words, heard again in the rustle of silk, some perverse reflection caused him to ask: 'What's the difference between a sari and a kimono?'

The lips of Mrs——'s mask trembled with agitation as she replied: 'The kimono is a gown.'

As soon as these words were out of her mouth, both he and she understood that it was over, that what was to have been said would not be said; and their excitation, having reached its climax, began to subside.

Reviewing the evening as he walked up the stairs, Borges did not reproach himself entirely. His despair was not unmixed when he realised that anyone could fail the difficult things. 'Yes,' he declared, as he opened the door to the study, 'the poignant thing is when we fail what should be easy.'

5.

Mrs—— liked to watch Borges sleeping. The deep lines of his large face showed as soft strips of shadow, and his sharp, angular body, now covered and curved like a bow, was as vulnerable as a gawky child's. She didn't pull the sheet back immediately. Rather, from a sheath beneath the bed, she withdrew a bone-handled stiletto whose silver blade gleamed like night water. It was only while he slept that Borges resembled her first husband, as if sleep, like an impossible alchemist, transformed all men into the same beautiful child. Mrs—— exposed the writer's back, and with the point of the blade, careful not to touch his skin, traced a line from his buttocks to his nape through the downy hair that grew along his spine. Borges stirred and smiled gently, but did not open his eyes. Mrs—— stared for some time at the soft flesh beneath his arm, but returned the polished knife to its sheath beneath the bed. Without disturbing the sleeping man, she lowered her gown to the floor and climbed in beside him.

Later that night, returning to her room, she removed the red vellum album from her desk and began to type, feverishly, but with a strange calm, as if she were already another woman. Borges, in spite of his impossible oblique-ness, had enabled her to see the whole. Her rapture was so intense she had almost forgotten the advertisements – had almost forgotten her reason for writing.

JANUARY 11, 1946   *10.10 P.M.*
It has got out of hand. I think my wife is poisoning me. If there is one principle I try to live by, it is that a man should always be prepared to accept what he holds to be impossible. My wife is a sensible woman, a gentle woman, I would even call her tolerant, but ever since I began withholding sexual favours from her, her behaviour has degenerated. I did expect some change (there would be no point to the exercise otherwise), but certainly nothing as marked

or extreme. About a month ago she disappeared for a couple of days, and when she returned, not a word. She was wearing a mask, but she did not say a word. I began to notice changes in myself. Small things to begin with: I'd break into a sweat over nothing, my feet would swell, and I started losing hair. I liked the idea of her going to see the witch, I wouldn't have thought of that, and I liked the mask too, but Christ, I'm finding it harder and harder to get out of bed. I've tried to explain, but she won't listen or talk to me any more, and she won't let me into her bed. I don't know how she's doing it. I eat nothing prepared by her, but every day it gets worse, and I don't know what to do. I can feel my strength going; I can no longer tell when I'm awake or asleep. I'm slipping away. There's nothing to hold onto and I'm slipping away.

JANUARY 12, 1946   11.00 A.M
There is no compromise in a relationship. There might be balance over many years, but in every issue one partner wins, the other loses. When the man or the woman starts to fight, it doesn't matter; the violence let loose has no memory, nor any sense of what's to come. It knows neither beginning nor end — the violence of long love is a fire that wants only to consume. In marriage, the only victories are Pyrrhic.

JANUARY 13, 1946   1.00 A.M.
My wife was a collector of cerebral men. I know this now. She lures them, she seduces them, and she kills them. She writes it all down. Like some demented Scheherazade. She's in bed now; I saw the light under the door. When I broke in she tried to hide the book, but I saw it. I asked her to give it to me. She looked away. I asked

again, louder this time. She stared at me, but wouldn't speak. I felt strong again. I walked across the room and grabbed at the book. She slapped me across the cheek. I grabbed her neck. I didn't want to kill her, but I couldn't stop. I felt strong again. I carried her to bed and covered her so I wouldn't have to look.

For a moment, while typing the last entry of her late husband's life, Mrs—— forgot to breathe. Now she breathed deeply and felt at peace. When she thought of Borges and his story it was in a past long ago, and for the first time in her life she experienced a memory as if it were distant. There was such joy in this sensation she would have liked to cry. Everything she had done, she knew it now, had been worth this one sensation, and was justified by it. Mrs—— had a life. When she stood up from the desk, she left the diary open where it lay. She would dispose of the old typewriter in the morning.

6.

Borges felt no shame at his failure; in fact, he felt liberated and strangely free. He still loved Mrs——, but with the melancholy beauty of an impossible love that knows no hope of fulfilment. He felt free to write, strangely free. It was as if (and the thought was exquisite) he didn't exist.

As with all his discoveries, the photographer discovered only by accident that ghosts, too, could die. He had never photographed the same ghost twice. This didn't bother him greatly, but it niggled away at him for so long that one morning he had already begun the experiment before he knew what it was that he was doing. The experiment was simple enough. While wandering around the museum (a particularly fertile source of ghosts) he took two shots of each painting in rapid succession. And sure enough, when he developed the film that evening, the one ghost he did unearth existed only in the first exposure. For a time he was disturbed by this discovery and tested it often. But on every occasion he met with the same result. Then one night, in a dream, he realised what was happening. The ghosts were living in purgatory and his photographs were setting them free.

Borges paused and looked around the room. He thought again of the night of his arrival. Of the woman, in a white silk shift as fine as gauze, so easy in her nakedness she made him feel exposed, and a mask as beautiful as any face he could imagine, moulded so closely to her skin it seemed to him alive. And it struck him, as she walked around the room, pointing out objects and relating their histories, while he followed, his arms folded nervously across his stomach, it struck him that he accepted it all, the mask and the advertisement and the pale buttocks moving before his eyes. He accepted it not as a mystery, but as something magical, something that had been vouchsafed him at the end of his life, for reasons he couldn't explain, didn't want to explain, because he loved the woman without a name, loved her without restraint, for this moment of carnal grace.

'I know your work,' she said, and recited:

Even the wind
Leaves its shadow
On the dunes.
Her footprints
Like an echo in sand.

'That was a long time ago,' Borges had said, unable to believe the words in her mouth were his own.

Mrs—— had not entered his room again. And what puzzled Borges, it was only after she left that he had felt her threat. She had touched his arm.

When the photographer picked up the paper that morning he was surprised to see a photograph of himself on the front page. It took him a moment to remember the incident in the park when he was assailed by the two journalists. He remembered how he had been photographed with his own camera, and had returned home and replaced the roll of film. He had thought that there was no reason to develop the shot, but he was overcome now by an unaccountable desire to do so. The haste with which he had replaced the film bothered him. He sipped his coffee, but was anxious and could not finish his breakfast. He was certain that he had thrown the film away, he hated clutter, but he was in such a state of agitation it was as if he were driven. He entered the darkroom, turned on the light, and began to search.

Borges had no sense of the quality of the writing; he no longer cared if it was good. He had seen the end and his only desire now was to reach it. He had never forgotten himself in a story before, and the sensation was so pleasing he experienced an instant of self-consciousness – a coruscation of the whole, gone before it is given. Borges tried to remember himself, the man he had been before he entered the woman's house, but in this glorious reverie of forgetting, he could remember nothing. He could see only Mrs—— reading the last lines of his story.

He found the roll, not in the darkroom, but in a small wicker basket he kept near his bed. His excitement subsided. Rather than develop the film immediately, he felt wonderfully calm in its possession. The days passed and although he had no thought of destroying the roll, he thought less and less about it. He knew where it was and that was good and that was enough. He no longer left the house. His desire to photograph ghosts had gone. He ate rarely and slept in bits. He dreamed now only of the film. At first the dreams were gentle, but as the weeks passed they grew into wild machines that left him scarred and broken on waking. He could remember none of the details, and felt only the dimmest apprehension of some terrible gift. He was wasting away. Then one night he woke, still and at peace, as if the machines had done their worst to him and could do no more, and he beheld the lucid traces of the dream. It was beautifully simple. He got out of bed and walked calmly to the darkroom. In the dark light he watched as first his face and then his hands became clear. He felt nothing but a strange pleasing terror. He knew that he was dead, that purgatory ceased the moment that he saw himself, but still he wondered, beyond all hope, if those hands, like a negative, spoke of a body disappeared, or a body just waiting to develop.

7.

Borges rose early. The sun had only just risen and he dressed in the pale blue light that filtered through the curtains. He felt light and at peace, pleasantly mournful, as if already nostalgic for what he was about to leave behind. After gathering the last pages of his story from the desk, he picked up the small suitcase he had packed before bed, and left the room.

In the dining room, even the table was now covered by a dustsheet. It was as if the house had not been lived in for many years, and Borges experienced a strange revulsion, as if an insect had just crawled across his skin. The air was stale and heavy. He placed the story on the sheeted chair which for the past month had been his own, and left the room quickly, his dread subsiding with the motion.

Mrs— rose early. The sun had only just risen and she dressed in the pale blue light that filtered through the curtains. She felt light and at peace, pleasantly mournful, as if already nostalgic for what she was about to leave behind. After gathering the last pages of her diary from the desk, she picked up the old typewriter she had wrapped before bed, and left the room.

In the dining room, even the table was now covered by a dustsheet. It was as if the house had not been lived in for many years, and Mrs— experienced a strange revulsion, as if an insect had just crawled across her skin. The air was stale and heavy. She placed the diaries on the sheeted chair which for the past month had been her own, and left the room quickly, her dread subsiding with the motion.

Outside, the morning
was quiet and still. He looked
up at what he believed to
be the woman's room, then
around him at the sculptured
gardens. No one. He hoped she
would understand the story.
It wasn't that he was afraid of
saying goodbye, more that he
hated repetition. He felt fresh
and alive. For the first time
since his arrival he had slept
without dreaming. And now,
in the giant shadow of the
house, he thought again of the
woman with the delicate man's
face, depthless and without
body, whirling through the
early morning light, dancing
to the tune of a Chopin waltz.
Borges turned and set off
down the gravel drive, his eyes
closed, giving himself up to
her feet.

Outside, the morning
was quiet and still. She looked
up at what she believed to
be the writer's room, then
around her at the sculptured
gardens. No one. She hoped he
would understand the diaries.
It wasn't that she was afraid of
saying goodbye, more that she
hated repetition. She felt fresh
and alive. For the first time
since her arrival she had slept
without dreaming. And now,
in the giant shadow of the
house, she thought again of the
man with the delicate woman's
face, depthless and without
body, whirling through the
early morning light, dancing
to the tune of a Chopin waltz.
Mrs—— turned and set off
down the gravel drive, her eyes
closed, giving herself up to
his feet.

STILL

Day moon
night rain –
dry beneath this roof of shadows

Morandi had not moved in over fifty years. The process had been a slow one, involuntary to begin, and more like a fading of the light than a shutting down, his senses growing in their refinement as he gradually ceased to move. With a simplicity born of years of contemplation, he stood on a table in his small studio in via Fondazza, gathering dust.

Standing at his easel, a yellow Persian bottle, a milk-glass ampoule, an Ovaltine tin and a porcelain jug gaze with the eyes of believers; and the innermost bones of the man, dead to all in their stillness, appear to the four objects in their most consoling guise: in their *everlasting* aspect.

No one was permitted to see the four objects at work. The

room was their world. A window opened onto the court-
yard and the backs of houses. Below was a small garden
which they tended lovingly. They had found Morandi at
the Montagnola market. They studied then arranged him
on the small table on top of a sheet of butcher's paper
where his position was carefully marked, the shadow drawn
in to emphasise it. They then marked their own position
carefully in chalk on the floor.

The yellow Persian bottle liked to read Leopardi at
night – *the silent, infinite passing of time* – but the Ovaltine
tin was more fond of Pascal, whose *Pensées* he would read
aloud to the others.

The eternity of things in themselves or in God must
still amaze our brief span of life. The fixed and constant
immobility of nature, compared to the continual changes
going on in us, must produce the same effect. And what
makes our inability to know things absolute is that they
are simple in themselves, while we are composed of two
opposing natures of different kinds, soul and body. For it is
impossible for the part of us which reasons to be anything
but spiritual, and even if it were claimed that we are simply
corporeal, that would still more preclude us from knowing
things, since there is nothing so inconceivable as the idea
that matter knows itself.

He liked the absurdity of that, that we might be simply
corporeal. For the Ovaltine tin, more than the others, never

ceased to be astonished by the beauty of his model, who could remain motionless for hours without speaking, like some necessary thing not needing to act in order to be, and who, always remaining in place, made him forget that time was passing.

The four objects had recently heard a story about a merchant from Parma who had come into possession of what he thought was one of their still-life paintings during the war. After the war the merchant happened to be in Milan and went into an art gallery where a group exhibition was being held. There he saw several of the four objects' work for the first time. He was astonished when, through heaven knows what illusory effect, he saw the subject in the paintings move and increase in size, and caught a glimpse of Morandi coming to life. Great was his disappointment back in Parma when he found that no matter how hard he concentrated on *his* painting, the subject remained completely motionless. Later it turned out that his still life was a forgery. The merchant went on to become a collector, buying paintings he selected from among those in which he 'saw things move'; the marvellous thing was that his special way of seeing a painting coincided with the opinion of the respected art critics.

What distinguished the style of the four objects more than anything else was their patience. They were essentially painters of the kind of still-life composition that communicates a sense of tranquility and privacy, moods which they valued above all else. As their friend, the poet Rafaello Franchi, once put it: 'No humble subject rendered marvellous by love was ever more ardently (if immaterially) touched than the man who was the four objects' model.'

And it is clear that the meaning of the four objects' still lifes is not to be found in the meaning of the man whom they painted. They deliberately chose the most ordinary man, who could not elicit in the mind of the viewer any instinctive response. In their studio Morandi divested himself of his disguise, his human function, and became their mirror. The paint became thinner, the colour translucent, and the sky full of light.

It takes time to get to things. One day, after many years of absence, Morandi's three sisters returned to the house in via Fondazza and entered their brother's studio. They were surprised by the clutter on the floor; a narrow path led from the door to the easel and from the easel to a faded divan – otherwise the floor was littered with bottles. They had no difficulty in recognising their brother; he was set as if on a miniature stage, and to their eyes he looked strangely false. Only in the canvasses stacked on the easel did he seem to possess a dignity and life of his own. In these paintings a transformation had occurred: their brother, now real, exulted in a sublime geometric space.

One of the sisters stepped close to her brother and raised her hand as if to brush the dust from his face and shoulders. But something in the gesture itself stilled her hand, a religious respect for something sacred, that *something infinite* that appears within every thing. She became aware that they had been speaking in whispers. She remembered her brother as a boy, attracted by the junk shop on the ground floor of the tenement house in which they lived. She remembered the hours he would spend in the shop, surrounded by the debris of human resignation, scraps and dregs imbued with humanity, as sacred as relics, which, coming into his bedroom late at night, she would see him tracing serenely in the air before he fell asleep.

TOYS

Yet thou hast made him little less than God

PSALMS

From the flat roof of the museum he could see the edge of the city and the silver harbour with its light. Klippel liked the night, the way darkness could reduce even infinite space to the dimensions of a small room, and his guilt was not without its pleasure when he thought again of the five years that had passed since he had stolen his first doll. He had worn the Spiderman suit that day as well. Still hadn't repaired the small cat's-eye tear he made in the knee crawling in through the toilet window. Even in the dark he could see the small triangle of pale scar tissue against the blue silk. He pushed his face against the pale glass of the skylight, scattering shadows across the museum floor.

The Spiderman suit was not a joke. He had made it

long before he started making the puppets that everyone thought of as sculptures. Not only was the red and blue silk like a second skin, it was in fact a continuation of nature, the kind of skin a line of thieves would evolve given enough time. The mask, with its great insect sockets, concealed even the shine of his eyes. But more important than camouflage was the intricate web of cords and pulleys he had devised that made him almost immune to gravity.

He shattered the skylight with the steel piton which hung by a thread from his belt. The echo was momentary, the glass fell onto the carpet beneath almost without a sound. Klippel lowered himself through the metal frame and dropped two body-lengths to the floor. He knew the building well; the tiny objects it contained were not considered of sufficient value to warrant any more than the most rudimentary protection. He removed a candle from a sheath against his shin. The museum presented him with little challenge, he could forgive it for that – but that the things he valued above all else in the world were considered practically worthless by those who possessed them, that he could not forgive. 'Unless the source of an object's beauty is appreciated,' speaking directly to the stone pedestals and glass display cabinets, 'it remains unowned; it remains, like you, in the terrible limbo of the damned.' For museums were nothing more than charnel-houses, and although he realised it would be hypocritical (as well as physically impossible) for him to remove every object (he was the first to acknowledge he did not appreciate the wonder of all that came from human hands), he considered it his mission to liberate those spirits whose beauty had touched his soul, and unlock the chains of their transmigration.

In the candle's sudden light he marvelled at the animal shapes, the dogs and swans and mantises that would not keep still, the flickering souls of stolid bronze busts, terracotta amphorae and amber necklaces, the secret animal life of the lazy inanimate world. Klippel was drawn to the shadows, reached out to touch their shallow nakedness, and would if he could have taken them in preference to the objects whose reality they confirmed. If the barbarians had any clue at all, he mused, it was the shadows they'd lock in glass cases. In his careful backward motion he brushed a toy Russian church and the gentle tintinnabulation of its tiny pitched bells was like an echo of its shadow's elephant sway. In the cupped light even his own head stretched and rippled across the ceiling like a giant amoeba. *'To save circumlocution,'* addressing the shadow this time, *'I shall call the doctrine that living matter may be produced by not-living matter, the hypothesis of Abiogenesis* – Professor Huxley addressing the British Association at Liverpool, September 1870. About what? Two Greek words: *bios* and *genesis*; birth without life; the origination of living organisms from lifeless matter. Well and good. But what would the learned Professor Huxley have to say about shadows? Organic or inorganic?' He looked down from the ceiling, his eyes on the flame. 'Would a biologist grant a shadow life? Surely, he must.'

The Clay Museum of Dolls and Statues, like the world, was divided arbitrarily, a great sprawling figtree of an arrangement that grew around the political whims of its curators and the vanities of its benefactors, but whose contingency had long since been forgotten as a taxonomy based on nation, and to a lesser extent history, had come to seem so inevitable as to be taken as nature itself. It was for this reason that Klippel was able to step out of Athens (a city?) into the Orient (a concept?) with no visible infringement of any physical law. He raised his arm to wedge the candle into the stone folds of a plump Buddha's neck and opened a huge shadow fan on the wall. 'So that's your game, my friend?' He assumed the pose of the warrior. Edging between the candle and the wall he watched the shadow swell and then diminish, holding his place when the faceless black figure shrank into his size. Because the Spiderman suit was tight to his body, the shadow was naked and anatomically precise, but due to the angle of the candle it did not provide a perfect simulacrum, and so gave him the illusion of an opponent outside himself.

Klippel turned side-on to the shadow. Transferring weight to his front leg, he began a sequence of fighting movements based on the twelve animals of Hsing-i, the purest of the Chinese soft martial arts. As he wove his body through the *kata*, his opponent changed from horse to tiger to monkey to bear, answering each form with a symmetry so precise it was as if they had discovered the choreography of the Way. Never before had he encountered such a perfect opponent, and as he performed each *kata* for the shadow, the swallow's steep swoop and the lightning peck of the cockerel, the shadow revealed to him the animal he had become. He fought with the focused beauty of a dancer. When finally he stopped and bowed to his opponent, he could hear nothing above his breathing. He sat down and the shadow disappeared into the wall.

The room looked different from the floor. Beneath the candle's halo he saw the dolls as if through water. He wondered if from above he might look the same to them, with the same elongated face, his two eyes merging at the bridge of his nose and his ears like narrow telephones. '*Sur,*' he thought, 'the view from above. That was the whole point of *surrealism*, surely?' Klippel loved playing with words almost as much as he loved making the sculptures that were his puppets, and when he got his teeth into an etymo-logical problem there was no telling where he might end. 'Why not *surprise*, then, as above the *prize*, and *surveillance* as above the *veil*? It makes sense. You *surrender* by placing yourself above the *render*, standing above the battlements and waving the white flag, and a *sermon* is above the *mon*, the old French priest leaving his lesson on the mantelpiece so it won't be lost before Sunday...' A small bird caught his eye. Even through the watery light it looked like the work of a taxidermist. He had nothing against the art of taxidermy, but in the world of dolls, to preserve something that had already been made, notwithstanding the pleasure of the illusion and the artistry of the craftsman, was to cheat.

He stood up to examine the bird more closely and smashed the glass lid of the case. Removing the bird from the bough on which it was perched, he could not contain his delight as his hand revealed what his eye had not seen; that he was, in fact, in the presence of a master. It was a yellow canary alright, but a canary born of silk, with claws and beak of painted wood and eyes of lapis lazuli, a canary more than three hundred years old. Each feather had been sewn individually, the counterfeit undetectable, and no two feathers were the same. As he raised the bird to the light its soft breast brushed his nose and released the faintest scent of sandalwood. He also felt a slight imbalance in the bird's slim neck. He'd read about such wonders before, dolls made for the children of Emperors and Shoguns, each bird taking more than a year to complete. But if the bird itself were a marvel, what it concealed was more marvellous still. Klippel cupped the canary in his right hand and with the fingers of his left hand tickled its throat. He heard the faint whirring of metal wheels and then the four notes of song, straining through the dark like water through cloth. And again the quietest trace of sandalwood, as if music were not enough and had to come scented like a flower. In a transport of delight he danced, stroking the bird's throat whenever the perfumed notes ceased.

It took some time to realise the sounds he was hearing were not made by the bird alone. Someone else had entered the museum. Klippel stopped. He put the bird back onto its perch and looked around the room.

How much had the intruder heard? He would have to work quickly now.

What he wanted was in a glass cylinder no taller than his arm. He had seen the kimono two nights before, and the slatted sandals. He loved the Japanese dolls more than anything in the museum, not so much for their immediate beauty as for the detail which was mostly hidden, which the doll's maker knew would be hidden, but on which he seemed to lavish even more care, as if in compensation for its invisibility. The tiny buds of the earlobes, hidden beneath a scarf's stiff folds or an ornately coiffured wig, carved, then sanded and rubbed with the sculptor's own spittle, burnished lightly, to give them the illusion of a raindrop's soft weight. The white lace socks, embroidered with Buddhist legend, hidden by the lacquered slippers. The damask collars, folded like paper boats, then starched and shaped to the neck, the fit so perfect they required no glue even beneath the heavy heraldic armour of the medieval warrior. Or the courtesans' elbows, which he had to lift the sleeves of their gowns to see, shaved from softwood and inserted like a joint into the rigid arm, but smooth as an egg and tattooed with the carver's name, as if he could make nothing more exquisite than this simple bone.

He took the Geisha from the glass cylinder and held her by the ankles. He turned his head away and undressed her quickly. He sniffed the black silk before folding the kimono carefully along its seams and attaching it to a clip at his waist. He removed the two tiny sandals, slipping his fingers beneath the soft leather straps. He returned the naked doll to its place and held the sandals up to the candle. They were a little smaller than his thumbs, but on the wall they became wings so large the room could not contain them. He let them chase each other across the walls as if rehearsing them for the puppets they would soon become, strangely poignant in their asymmetry. He became aware of the sound again, but as before, only after it had passed. On the ceiling the striped wings merged then plunged like a kite. He slipped the sandals into a small stomach pouch beneath the webbing of his suit. 'I know what you're up to,' he whispered. 'You think the Spiderman's prone to hallucinations, that you can deceive him into believing that you are no more than a creaking shadow.' He doused the candle. Retraced his steps through the Orient to the outskirts of Athens. The rope hung where he had left it. He pulled himself up and through the broken skylight, stood in silence on the roof of the museum, looking out across the city to the dark skin of the harbour.

A light caught his eye. In an apartment building across the road from the museum a woman stood at an open window, backlit by a shaded lamp that stood by a bed. She was looking straight at him, but with a vacancy that did not include him. He enjoyed being inside her gaze; it relaxed him, somehow, and he paused, looking back at the woman. She stood so still he could almost have forgotten he was now outside the museum. She was wearing a heavy quilted dressing gown, but he could see the lace collar of her nightdress in the space where the top button had torn away. The elbows of the gown were worn to transparency, as if the woman stood often like this at her window, bent over the city, but never seeing it. Klippel searched for her ears. Her hair was short and frizzled with sleep, but although the sides of her head were clearly visible he couldn't see her ears. For an instant he felt a terrible vertigo, as if something inside himself was falling and he was falling after it, unable to catch it or pull it back. The woman had gone, and her window had become one dark rectangle among many. Trembling, he looked at the building, so austere in its geometry; nine black rectangles, evenly spaced, in three parallel rows. He couldn't get over the sense that somehow he had been looking, not at the woman, but through her to the room beyond, and that nailed to the wall above the bed were two small ears, white as flowers, trickling blood. Lowering himself down the wall into the darkness, he gave himself up to the rhythm of descent and disappeared into the night.

RAGS

Another poet whom the angels guide, cherish and torment is Erik Satie, who walks every night from Montmartre or Montparnasse to his home at Arcueil-Cachan — a miracle which cannot be explained unless the angels carry him...

JEAN COCTEAU

1. *Gnossiene (Avec une tristesse rigoureuse)*

Now everyone came out of the church. At the church door stood an old crippled soldier leaning on a crutch. Just as Suzanne Valadon was lifting her foot to get into her carriage the old soldier said: 'Dear me, what pretty dancing shoes!' and Suzanne could not help it, she was obliged to dance a few steps; and when she had once begun, her legs continued to dance. She danced round the church corner and could not stop; the coachman had to run after her and seize her and lift her into the carriage. But still her feet continued to dance. At last she took off her shoes, and her legs were at rest.

At home she threw the shoes into a cupboard, but she could not help looking at them and it wasn't long before they were on her feet again. She danced far out into the dark wood. She was frightened now, and wanted to throw the shoes away, but they had grown fast to her feet. She danced out into the open churchyard. She would have liked to sit down on the pauper's grave where the bitter fern grows, but for her there was neither peace nor rest. As she danced past the open church door she saw an angel there in long white robes, with wings reaching from his shoulders down to the floor; his face was stern and grave and in his hand he held a broad shining sword.

'Dance you shall,' said he, 'dance till you are pale and cold, till your skin shrivels up and you are a skeleton!'

'Mercy!' cried Suzanne. But she did not hear what the angel answered, for the shoes carried her through the gate into the fields. They bore her away over thorns and stumps till she was torn and bleeding; she danced away over the heath to a lonely little house. Here, she knew, lived the executioner.

'I don't suppose you know who I am?' the executioner said. 'I strike off the heads of the wicked, and I notice that my axe is tingling now.'

'Don't cut off my head,' said Suzanne. 'Cut off my feet with the red shoes.'

And then she confessed all her sins, and the execut-ioner cut off her feet with the red shoes, and the shoes danced away with the little feet across the field into the deep forest. And he carved her a pair of wooden feet so that she might follow the shoes wherever they danced before her.

2. *Mémoires d'un amnésique*

One morning, walking close by his home at Arcueil-Cachan, Erik Satie came across a scrap of manuscript paper on the side of the road. He was a solitary man and so not in the least bit surprised when he read the notes on the page and saw that they were solitary too, impossible to connect with anything familiar. He had never seen music like it, so apathetic – not antipathetic, which is a different matter – to humanity. Only a remarkable personality, he thought, could attain such impersonality and transform it into sound. He took the scrap of manuscript home and translated the musical notation into the following miniature.

At that time I was interested in alchemy. Alone in my laboratory one day I was resting. Outside, a leaden sky, livid and sinister.

I was feeling mournful, without knowing why; almost afraid, though for no apparent reason. It then occurred to me to amuse myself by counting on my fingers, slowly, from one to 260,000.

This I did, but I only succeeded in becoming more bored. Rising from my chair I went to take a magic nut and put it carefully in a casket of alpaca bone. Immediately a stuffed bird flew out; a monkey's skeleton ran away; a sow's skin climbed up the wall. Then night descended, covering everything up and abolishing shapes.

But someone is knocking on the door. What can it be? Oh God! do not abandon thy servant. He has certainly sinned, but now he repents. Pardon him, I beseech thee. Now the door is opening, opening – opening like an eye; a silent, shapeless creature is coming nearer, coming nearer...Out of the shadows comes a voice: 'Sir, I think I must have second sight.'

I do not recognise this voice. It goes on: 'Sir, it is I, it is only I.' 'Who are you?' I mutter in terror. 'It is I, your servant. I think I must have second sight. Did you place with care a magic nut in a casket of alpaca bone? And did immediately a stuffed bird fly out; a monkey's skeleton run away; and a sow's skin climb up the wall?' Suffocated, I can only answer: 'Yes, my friend. But how do you know?' He draws nearer, gliding darkly through the night. I can feel him trembling. No doubt he is afraid I am going to shoot him. Then, with a sob, like a little child, he murmurs: 'I saw you through the keyhole.'

3. *Musique d'ameublement*

Travellers from every country came to the city of the emperor, which they admired very much, as well as the palace and gardens; but when they heard the nightingale, they all declared it to be the best of all. And the travellers, on their return home, related what they had seen, and learned men wrote books.

The books travelled all over the world, and some of them came into the hands of the emperor, and he sat in his golden chair, and, as he read, he nodded his approval at every moment, for it pleased him to find such a beautiful description of his city, his palace and his gardens. But when he came to the words, 'the nightingale is the most beautiful of all', he exclaimed, 'What is this? I know nothing of any nightingale.'

Then he called one of his lords-in-waiting. 'There is a very wonderful bird mentioned here, called a nightingale,' he said. 'They say it is the best thing in my kingdom. Why have I never been told of it?'

'I have never heard the name,' replied the lord. 'She has not been presented at court.'

'It is my pleasure that she shall appear this evening,' the emperor said. 'The whole world knows what I possess better than I do myself.'

But where was the nightingale to be found? The nobleman went up stairs and down, through halls and passages, yet none of those whom he met had heard of the bird. At last he met with a little girl in the kitchen who said, 'Oh, yes, I know the nightingale quite well; she can, indeed, sing.' So she went into the wood where the nightingale sang, and half the court followed her.

And presently the nightingale began to sing. 'Hark! there she is,' the girl said. 'And there she sits.' She pointed to a little grey bird who was perched on a bough.

'Is it possible?' the lord asked. 'I never imagined it would be a little, plain, simple thing like that. She has certainly changed colour at seeing so many grand people around her.'

'My excellent little nightingale,' said the courtier. 'I have the great pleasure of inviting you to a court festival this evening.'

'My song sounds best in the green wood,' said the bird, but still she came willingly when she heard the emperor's wish.

That night the nightingale sang so sweetly that tears came into the emperor's eyes. 'That singing is a wonderful gift,' said the ladies of the court to each other, and they took water in their mouths to make them utter the gurgling sounds of the nightingale when they spoke, so that they might fancy themselves nightingales.

The nightingale was now to remain at court, to have her own cage, with liberty to go out twice a day, and once during the night. Twelve servants were appointed to attend her on these occasions, who each held her by a silken string fastened to her leg. There was certainly not much pleasure in this kind of flying. The whole city spoke of the wonderful bird.

One day the emperor received a large packet on which was written, 'The Nightingale'. Inside was an artificial nightingale made to look like a living one. As soon as the artificial bird was wound up, it could sing like the real one, and could move its tail up and down, which sparkled with silver and gold.

'This is very beautiful. Now they must sing together,' said the court. 'And what a duet it will be.' But they did not get on well, for the real nightingale sang in its own way, but the artificial bird sang only waltzes.

'That is not a fault,' said the music master, 'it is quite perfect to my taste.' So it was made to sing alone and then was as successful as the real bird, and so much prettier to look at, for it sparkled like bracelets and breast-pins. Over and over it sang the same tunes without being tired; the people would gladly have heard it again, but the emperor said the real nightingale ought to sing something. But where was she? No one had noticed her when she flew out of the open window, back to her own green woods.

'What strange conduct,' the emperor said, when her flight had been discovered, and all the courtiers blamed her and said she was an ungrateful creature.

'But we have the best bird of all,' said one, and then they would have the bird sing again, although it was the hundredth time they had listened to the same piece.

The music master praised the wind-up bird in the highest degree, and asserted that it was better than a real nightingale, not only in its dress, but also in its musical power. 'For you must perceive, my chief lord and emperor, that with a real nightingale we can never tell what is going to be sung, but with this bird everything is settled. It can be opened and explained, so that people may understand how the waltzes are formed, and why one note follows upon another.'

And everyone agreed.

WRINKLES

Philosophy ought really to be written as a poetic composition

LUDWIG WITTGENSTEIN

1   Things are as they are.

1.1   Comparison is essential to an understanding of how they are.

1.2   The problem of time may be approached thus: The old turtle was slow, but this was of no concern to her. What use had she for speed when she carried her home wherever she went, clinging like a baby to her back?

1.21   At first, when she was young, she felt it as a burden, this heavy shell that kept her out of games. But when the lizards who laughed at her clumsy gait disappeared in the mouths of greedy gulls and she alone was spared, she began to look at her burden in a different light.

1.22   Not only did it protect her from the jaws of preda-
tors, its weight, by slowing her to the pace of the sun across
the sky, enabled her to see the world in minutest detail. The
subtle beauty denied those who lived their lives at speed.

1.23   For the turtle had learnt the secret of time. She had
discovered that even life could be slowed until age ate no
more quickly than a river a rock.

1.3   Of W., however, I will only say that he grew into a
rather morose young man, always withdrawn into himself.
He began to show very early, almost in infancy – so,
at least, it was said – quite an extraordinarily brilliant
aptitude for learning.

1.31   During his first two years of university he was forced
to earn his own living as well as carry on with his studies.

1.311   It should be noted that he was born into one of the
wealthiest families in Europe yet liked to think of himself
as Ivan Karamazov. For that reason – was it pride? – during
that time he did not even attempt to enter into a correspondence with his father.

1.312   In spite of everything he succeeded in getting work,
at first by giving lessons at sixpence an hour, and then

by selling short 'stories' of street incidents to different newspapers under the signature of 'Eyewitness'.

1.313 These stories, it was said, were always so interestingly and pungently written that they were soon in great demand, and having got an entry into the editorial offices, he never lost touch with them.

1.32 During his last years at the university he began to publish brilliant reviews of books on various specialised subjects, so that he became well known even in literary circles.

1.321 It was only quite recently, however, that he happened to have succeeded in attracting the special attention of a much wider public.

2 In a proposition a world is as it were put together experimentally. (As when in the law court in Paris a motor-car accident is represented by means of dolls, etc.)

2.1 The old turtle had given birth to so many green turtles she could no longer count them, let alone remember them by age.

2.11 Each year, when she came ashore to scoop out holes in the island sand beyond the reach of the tide and deposit there her score of leathery eggs, each year, after scraping the sand back over the eggs and tamping it firm, she would gather around her the hundred generations of her family and together they would wait while the sun hatched the eggs around them.

2.12   For those who escaped the beaks of the gulls, scrambling to the water through the diving shadows, time too would stop for them – powerless before the miracle that built itself upon their backs.

2.2   First of all let me say that this young man, W., was not at all a fanatic and, at least in my opinion, not even a mystic.

2.21   If he were a mystic, he was a mystic for whom certainty of a kind existed – the certainty of unknowing.

2.3   He liked to think of himself as Alyosha Karamazov, a precocious lover of humanity.

2.31   If he took up the monastic way of life it was only because at the time it appealed powerfully to his imagination and showed him, as it were, the ideal way, an escape for his soul which was struggling to emerge from the darkness of worldly wickedness to the light of love.

2.32   Still, I do not deny that he was very strange even then.

3   The general form of a proposition is: This is how things are. That is the kind of proposition one repeats to oneself countless times. One thinks that one is tracing the outline of the thing's nature over and over again, and one is merely tracing round the frame through which we look at it.

3.1   In his childhood and adolescence he was not effusive and he did not even like to talk a great deal, but it was not from mistrustfulness, nor from shyness; quite the contrary, it was from something else, from a sort of inner preoccupation, a preoccupation that concerned only himself and had nothing to do with anyone else, but was so important to him that he seemed to forget others because of it.

3.11   He remembered an evening, a quiet summer evening, an open window, the slanting rays of the setting sun (it was the slanting rays that he remembered most of all), an icon in the corner of the room, a lighted lamp in front of it, and on her knees before the icon his mother, sobbing as though in hysterics, snatching him up in her arms, hugging him to her breast so tightly that it hurt, and praying for him to the Virgin, holding him out in both arms to the icon as though under the Virgin's protection, and suddenly a nurse runs in and snatches him from her in terror.

3.2   The results of philosophy are the uncovering of one or another piece of plain nonsense and of bumps that the understanding has got by running its head up against the limits of language. These bumps make us see the value of the discovery.

3.21 We never arrive at fundamental propositions in the course of our investigation; we get to the boundary of language which stops us from asking further questions. We don't get to the bottom of things, but reach a point where we can go no further, where we cannot ask further questions.

3.3 It was on one of these occasions that a large frill-necked lizard sidled up to the turtle on the wrack line and began taunting her.

3.31 When are you going to die? the lizard said. Why won't you surrender gracefully, like the rest of us, and give up this shameful cheating of time?

3.32 The turtle had dealt with jealous lizards before. I've never heard anyone call age a sin. I'm sorry if it disturbs you. But it's not easy, you know. You see and hear a lot of things, not all of them good. And you can't get rid of them. They weigh heavier than any shell. Believe me, it's I who should be jealous of you.

3.33 Me, jealous? Why would anyone want to be like you?

3.34   Then let's see what you have to say to this, the turtle continued, thinking to teach the lizard a lesson. You think I'm so old and slow? Let's have a race, then. Once around the island. If you beat me, I'll take my own life and die gracefully as you suggest. But if I win, you'll have to carry me on your back for the rest of your life. What do you say?

3.35   If you're so stupid to challenge me, the young frillneck sneered, you don't deserve to live. Name your time.

3.36   This afternoon, before sunset. The turtle smiled, imagining the outcome of her plan. We can start and finish by this palm tree.

3.4   What we find out in philosophy is trivial; it does not teach us new facts, only science does that. But the proper synopsis of these trivialities is enormously difficult, and has immense importance. Philosophy is in fact the synopsis of trivialities.

3.41   So in the end, when one is doing philosophy, one gets to the point where one would like just to emit an inarticulate sound.

4   Surely one *cannot* will one's own destruction, and anybody who has visualised what is in practice involved in the act of suicide knows that suicide is always a *rushing of*

one's own defences. But nothing is worse than to be forced to take oneself by surprise. Undoubtedly, it is the knowledge of death, and therewith the consideration of the suffering and misery of life, that give the strongest impulse to philosophical reflection and metaphysical explanations of the world.

4.01   The lizard ran off, anxious to tell the whole island about the race he was certain of winning and the strange prize that would be his. The turtle could feel nothing but sorrow for a creature who derived so much excitement from the prospect of such a victory.

4.011 But her sorrow was not only for the young lizard. She couldn't forget what he had said. For the first time in her life she felt her age, and to her horror found that she could no longer remember what it was like to be young.

4.012 She became aware that for some time life had been a burden she refused to admit to herself, preferring instead to see the weight entirely in terms of her shell, like a military uniform. But it was the uniform of a force that no longer existed. She belonged to a past age.

4.02   My work is the work of an old man: for, though I am not really old, I have, somehow, an old soul. May it be granted to me that my body doesn't survive my soul.

4.021 Having graduated from the university and preparing

to leave for abroad, W. published in one of the leading newspapers a strange article, which attracted the attention of a large audience, on a subject on which he was apparently not an expert.

4.022 The article dealt with a theological question which was being widely debated at the time. After discussing several opinions which had already been published on this subject, he went on to express his own view.

4.023 What was so striking about his article was its tone and its extraordinarily surprising conclusion.

4.024 And yet many churchmen were convinced that its author was on their side.

4.025 But quite unexpectedly, not only secularists but even atheists expressed their agreement with his views.

4.026 In the end several shrewd persons decided that the whole thing was nothing but an impertinent practical joke.

4.03 A theology which insists on the use of *certain particular* words and phrases, and outlaws others, does not make anything clearer. It gesticulates with words, as one might say, because it wants to say something and does not know how to express it.

5   Our desires conceal from us even what we desire.

5.1   The turtle gathered her family around her. After relating her plan for the race, she lumbered to the start. As on so many days and years before this one she waited, quiet and alone, by the sea that so often took her weight, while the sun clawed its way through the heavens.

5.11   Gradually, as the afternoon wore on, a crowd of animals gathered around the starting line. They had all come to laugh at her, the turtle thought, and watch her die.

5.12   Are you ready? the lizard laughed as he walked up to the palm tree that marked the beginning and the end of the course. Let's get it over with.

5.13   Beneath the cloud of sand thrown up by the lizard's whirling legs, the turtle trundled off to the palm tree where she hid and waited. When the whirlwind finally subsided the crowd gasped to see the frill-neck racing upright on his two hind legs not in front of, but behind the turtle. The muffled snorts of disbelief made the turtle smile to herself.

5.2   All his life W. seemed to have complete faith in people, and yet no one ever took him for a simpleton or a naïve person. There was something in him that told you and indeed convinced you (and it was so all through his life afterwards) that he did not want to set himself up as a judge of people, that he would not like to assume the role of one who condemned.

5.21 He liked to say that wisdom is cold and to that extent stupid.

5.211 Faith on the other hand is a passion.

5.22 But then, everyone loved this young man wherever he made an appearance, and that had been so from the earliest days of his childhood.

5.221 His gift of arousing a special kind of love in people was inherent in his very nature, artless and spontaneous.

5.222 It was the same at school, and yet it would seem that he was one of those children who arouse the distrust of their schoolmates and are sometimes laughed at and even hated.

5.223 For instance, he would often fall into a reverie and he seemed to shun the company of others. Even as a little boy he liked to retire into some corner and read a book. He was seldom playful or even merry, but one look at him was sufficient to make people realise that there was not a trace of despair in him; that, on the contrary, he was serene and even-tempered.

5.224 He never attempted to show off before children of

his own age. Perhaps that was why he was never afraid of anyone. His schoolfellows realised at once that he was not at all proud of his fearlessness, but gave the impression of someone who had no idea that he was brave or fearless.

5.3   There was only one trait of his character which invariably aroused in all his schoolmates from the lowest to the highest form the desire to pull his leg, though not out of malice but because it amused them. This was his absurd and morbid modesty and chastity.

6   My work consists of two parts: of the part which is here, and of everything which I have *not* written. And precisely this second part is the important one. For the ethical is delimited from within, as it were, by my book; and I'm convinced that, strictly speaking, it can ONLY be delimited in this way. In brief, I think: All of that which many are babbling today, I have defined in my book by remaining silent about it. Therefore the book will, unless I'm quite wrong, have much to say which you want to say yourself, but perhaps you won't notice that it is said in it.

6.1   I will tell you another anecdote, a very interesting and most characteristic anecdote about Herr W. It was only in philosophy that his creativity could truly be awakened, only then did one see wild life striving to erupt in him. For W., sensuality and philosophical thought were inextricably linked.

6.2   Five days ago, at a certain social gathering consisting mostly of ladies, he solemnly declared during an argument that there was absolutely nothing in the world to make men love their fellow men, that there was no law in nature that man should love mankind, and that if love did exist on earth, it was not because of any natural law but solely because men believed in immortality.

6.21   He added in parenthesis that all natural law consisted of that belief, and that if you were to destroy mankind's belief in immortality, not only love but every living force on which the continuation of all life in the world depended, would dry up at once.

6.22   Moreover, there would be nothing immoral then, everything would be permitted.

6.23   But that is not all: he wound up with the assertion that for every individual, like myself, for instance, who does not believe in God or his own immortality, the moral laws of nature must at once be changed into the exact opposite of the former religious laws, and that self-interest, even if it were to lead to crime, must not only be permitted but even recognised as the necessary, the most rational, and practically the most honourable motive for a man in my position.

6.24   From this paradox, you can conclude what sort of ideas our dear eccentric and paradoxical fellow has been propounding and, no doubt, will go on propounding in future.

6.3   The turtle's deception was beautifully simple. She knew the lizard would throw up clouds of sand as he ran and that these would provide perfect cover. Each time the lizard thought he had overtaken the turtle, from the cloud clearing around him another turtle would emerge to take the lead, lumbering out from behind the ring of palm trees that marked the perimeter of the course. At the first tree was the turtle's son, then her grandson after that, her great-grandson after him, and so on, the line stretching through time back to the old turtle who would step forth from the lizard's final cloud to cross the finish line victorious.

6.31   And the plan was working. Each time the frill-neck overtook what he believed to be the turtle, there she was, in front of him again, like a shadow, impossible to put behind. The faster he ran the further he fell behind until, exhausted by rage and frustration, the finish line in sight, he kicked up such a storm of sand that the old turtle was able to lumber onto the race track unnoticed. As the dust settled, she raised one of her splayed legs to the crowd, and crossed the line the winner. The lizard, head dragging in the sand, his face hidden behind the inflated crown of his neck, slunk up to the turtle through the nightmare of his shame.

6.32 Don't worry, the turtle said to him. What I'm feeling now is prize enough for me.

7 The philosopher's treatment of a question is like the treatment of an illness.

7.1 Anyone who had only the slightest acquaintance with W. was convinced that he was one of those men who in a way resembled saintly fools and who, if they suddenly came into possession of a large sum of money, would not hesitate to give it away at the first demand either to some charity or perhaps simply to the first clever swindler who happened to ask for it. And, generally speaking, he did not seem to know the value of money. Here you had perhaps the only man in the world who, if he were left alone without a penny in a strange city of a million inhabitants, would never die of exposure or hunger because he would instantly be fed and given some job, and if not, would find a job himself. His employer would consider it an honour.

7.2 Afterwards the lizard said to those who had seen, that it was something in the way she spoke, the look of sympathy and forgiveness, that made him snap. For after the turtle had spoken, he was on her in an instant. Before she had time to call to her family for help, the frill-neck ripped her from her carapace and left her, for the first time since hatching, naked of her shell. She didn't notice the laughter of the crowd, nor her frightened family as they gathered about her and guided her to a cave jutting out above the sea, so intoxicated was she by the sense of lightness. For hundreds of years she had carried her home, the whole world it seemed, on her back, and now at last she was free. Now I can die, she thought. She felt so light, only the roof of the cave stopped her floating away.

8　　What can be said at all can be said clearly; and whereof one cannot speak thereof one must be silent. There is indeed the inexpressible. This *shows* itself; it is the mystical. The nonsense that results from trying to say what can only be shown is not only logically untenable, but ethically undesirable.

8.1　　In the quiet solitude that comes with night when fear has changed to wonder and every thought is like a dream, the turtle stepped out of the frayed skirt of her lower shell. Time stroked her skin until it tingled with the touch and seemed to melt, poured through the cave like wax that time took in its calloused hands to crease and fold, slow like the night, first the turtle's knotted hands and feet, then the arms and gnarled legs, a body which was as the sand that holds the ghost of the sea in its wrinkles. The bent figure crept forth from the cave and hobbled across the hard uneven path of sleeping turtles away at last from the sea.

9   The *truth* of the thoughts that I have here communicated seems to me unassailable and definitive, and I believe myself to have found, on all essential points, the solution to the problems of philosophy. But if I am not mistaken in this belief, then the second thing in which the value of this work consists, is that it shows how little is achieved when these problems are solved.

CAGED

*In Zen they say if something is boring after two minutes,
try it for four*

3

On English going Sicily Tunis North I taken cheapest and was voyage two and day. were sooner of harbour I that my no was I a to captain I'd to to class. sent note saying could change further, whether had vaccinated. wrote that had been and I intend be. wrote that I vaccinated would be We meanwhile into terrific The were than boat. was to on deck. correspondence the and continued deadlock. my note him, stated firm to off boat the opportunity without vaccinated. then back I been and prove he along certificate his

signature with a sent it to, vaccinated had that wrote He being and earliest at his get intention my I to last In in myself captain between The the walk impossible It the

higher waves. storm a gotten had. permitted not I was
unless back He to didn't that vaccinated not I back I been
I asking, and not I back a He another change like saying
the note send. served food class in found than the out no
We one nights of a it passage the had. Africa in to from
boat an

1

4

       Siracusa in

               I was

  at Tunis

                  to disembark

2

I sit and wait for words that might resemble silence. Outside, the tree in which the blackbird sings does not exist. The blackbird, too, does not exist, but how can he say?

MAGIC

Many things on earth are hidden from us, but in return for that we have been given a mysterious, inward sense of our living bond with the other world, with the higher, heavenly world, and the roots of our thoughts and feelings are not here but in other worlds. That is why philosophers say that it is impossible to comprehend the essential nature of things on earth. God took seeds from other worlds and sowed them on this earth, and made his garden grow, and everything that could come up came up, but what grows lives and is alive only through the feeling of its contact with other mysterious worlds; if that feeling grows weak or is destroyed in you, then what has grown up in you will also die. Then you will become indifferent to life and even grow to hate it. That is what I think.

FYODOR DOSTOYEVSKY
'DISCOURSES AND SERMONS OF FATHER ZOSSIMA'

SCENE 1

The woman who served Fyodor Dostoyevsky coffee had a small tattoo on her left shoulder-blade. She was Polynesian, in her mid-thirties, with a face flawed enough to be beautiful and the figure of an athlete no longer in training, muscles gone flabby and voluptuous. Dostoyevsky thought of her often as he drove through the city at night, of the tattoo as she bent to spoon out ice-cream, visible beneath the thin strap of a halter-neck blouse.

SCENE 2

The prostitutes in cheap camisoles and braided leather cowboy boots looked young when seen from a distance. They bobbed like seagulls just far enough from the shining entrances to the clubs, their eyes beseeching yet averted. Dostoyevsky hated crossing the road. The girls aged a lifetime in a step.

SCENE 3

The room was shaped like an amphitheatre. The stage floor and its three walls were covered with mirror-tiles which glinted in the footlights; it was as if the dancers made love to themselves, not as a whole, but frantically, in parts. Dostoyevsky was glad he was known. He pushed his way carefully to the bar at the rear of the room, his head made light by the haze of smoke and perfume, and the endless nights without sleep. He ordered a vodka and sat in the corner. A woman seemed to take shape from a cloud of smoke.

SCENE 4

A hapless club magician, barely visible on the stage, bowed. Dostoyevsky had not seen him before. He had, on the table in front of him, what appeared to be the layers of an onion. His bony hands shook. Even the strippers came out from behind the stage. They stood with their backs to the audience, laughing at the man, their bottoms wobbling like jellies in the muted light.

SCENE 5

A face and long scarred hands, hovering at the ends of a cloak. It was as if his body were the trick. He had pulled

a rabbit out from beneath his cloak but it had broken free
from his grasp. Each time he reached out to catch it, the
rabbit jumped just beyond the reach of his hands.

SCENE 6
God came to Fyodor Dostoyevsky in the kitchen of his
Stanley Street terrace the following morning. Dostoyevsky
spooned out the kidneys he was frying onto a piece of
unbuttered toast and sat down at the table. He had not seen
God in the kitchen before. He cut carefully a corner of the
toast and dipped it in the almost clear juice before putting
it into his mouth. He closed his eyes and chewed. Sleep had
all but abandoned him at night, but in the hollows between
tosses he dreamed. Sydney at last fell quiet. Only in the
small reserve across the street from his house, desolate with
rubbish as anonymous as the drifting junk of the sea, was
there the occasional gasp of he knew not what emotion and
the muzzled murmuring of dogs, half-asleep like himself.

SCENE 7
'I'm still here.' God spoke with the weary patience of a
father. 'My son has returned.' Dostoyevsky refused to open
his eyes. He chewed slowly and without thought, trying
to catch what was left of his dream, where Jesus had just
raised Lazarus from the dead but Lazarus was not happy.
His wife had remarried. The prostitutes he visited shrank
from him in terror. And everyone looked at him as if there
was something wrong. Even his sisters wouldn't sit at the

169

same table. He could feel them pinching him in his sleep. And to top it all off, the high priests were plotting his death, because on account of him the Jews were starting to believe in Jesus. 'What have you got against me?' God sat down at the table and picked up a kidney from the plate, eyeing it like a child before putting it into his mouth. His body became apparent only when he needed to use it, and even then, it was only the functioning part that took on any substance. He was all mouth and stomach. 'I'm not going until you talk to me.'

SCENE 8

Through the window, rain was pouring off the roof so hard it seemed to hang in the air like spaghetti. It didn't make a sound. Dostoyevsky emptied his plate into a small plastic bucket beneath the sink. 'Why is it in *Matthew*, and then again at the end of *Mark*, why is it that faith's required to gain eternal life? Jesus doesn't ask us to be good. He orders us to believe. Why are you so worried that we won't believe in you?'

'People don't want the resurrection.' God rose to his feet and paced nervously around the kitchen, his mouth, hands and legs seemingly unconnected, yet moving in perfect accord. 'They don't want to believe in what they can see. Where's the excitement in that? No one wants proof of his faith. The martyrs, you know what they prayed for? Their secret hope was that I didn't exist. And people call me a masochist.' God laughed and Dostoyevsky turned to face him again. 'If you find the Grail, what are you going to do after that, Fyodor? Have a cup of tea?'

'How do I know you're not the Other, come to deceive me?' Dostoyevsky smiled, remembering the mad conversations he'd had with his father.

'For a long time I didn't even know I was God. Can you imagine what that's like, to be God and not to know it...the loneliness? What if mortality were a gift? You can at least kill yourself. I can do anything but be like you...'

SCENE 9

He put on his beret and coat, and wrapping a scarf around his neck, *walked out into the St Petersburg morning. The sky had cleared, the sun was black, and the light was pale with winter. But there was no snow.* A few leaves blew in flurries around the roots of the blue gums. Two boys kicked a soft drink can against the gutter. He closed the door and rubbed his hands against the grey sandstone wall.

SCENE 10

'James the martyr, surnamed the Dismembered, came of Christian parents, and was married to a Christian wife; but he allowed himself to be beguiled by his great love of the king, and began to worship the idols. When his mother and wife learned of this, they wrote to him, saying, "By obeying a mortal man, you have exchanged truth for falsehood. Know, therefore, that we shall be strangers to you, nor shall we ever again dwell with you..."'

The passenger in the back seat of the taxi coughed and Dostoyevsky remembered where he was.

'Sorry,' he said, trying to fix the man's face in the rear-vision mirror. 'It gets better...With a family like that, you'd welcome the burning coals. So, James listened to the words of his wife and mother and agreed to die like all the rest...But you know who I feel sorry for in all of this – it's the torturers who really suffer. They have to put James to death so he can be a martyr, but God doesn't love them for it and history despises them. It's the same with Judas. James laughs at them and goads them on, he calls on them to make him great, and sends them all to hell. They're the true martyrs...'

'Absolute rulers want to be loved.' The passenger's voice, though perfectly clear, seemed to come from outside the car. 'That's why the martyrs angered them so much. And to top it off, they refused to fear.'

Dostoyevsky loved an argument and couldn't believe his luck. He slowed the taxi to a crawl, praying for red lights. 'What they did was easy...Hypocrites, all of them. Torment my body which torments me. There's nothing special about that. They were just good at promoting themselves. Sensualists, cultivating their own humiliation. The devil kindled in St Dominic such a fire of passion for a woman, he had to strip off his clothes and roll in the thorns and brambles until his whole body was lacerated. As if denial isn't the greatest form of lust...They hate the world because they hate themselves, and in their fear they call on God to destroy us all…'

'You seem to know a lot about them…'

Dostoyevsky stopped speaking, puzzled by the voice. The man had lowered his head. His face was hidden. He brushed the hair away from his eyes, and his hands were like the solution to a problem the driver became aware of only now that it had been solved.

SCENE 11

Dostoyevsky looked out of the taxi. By day the strip clubs seemed to him as lions without teeth; the prostitutes walked the street without make-up and a young policeman, no more than a boy, watched the derelicts as they slept on the wooden benches of Fitzroy Gardens. He wondered how it was that something as simple as a change of light could so transform a place, while behind his passenger, through the rear window of his taxi flecked with birdshit, the massive glass towers of the city loomed, making a thousand suns.

SCENE 12

The café was always busy on a Saturday night. The old Italian men sat in the corner beneath the long counter, drinking coffee from small white cups and playing cards. On the wall above their heads, as if through mist, Dostoyevsky could see the dirty baroque churches, the quiet fishing villages and the mountain peaks, framed like windows and always with a woman in front, as if human beauty grew from history or the dark Italian soil as naturally as the hills and clouds and sea. He turned and saw the small tattoo, its edge just visible beneath the sleeve which, in all the activity, had ridden up past the woman's shoulder. He looked at the ice-cream melting in the shining metal cups. Young men, their heads like Chinese gooseberries, dressed in black jeans tucked into long black boots, shouted orders across the counter. Dostoyevsky looked up from the plastic jars filled with chocolates wrapped in coloured foil, and the cross-cakes and cannoli stacked neatly on trays beside the towers of clean cups and saucers, to the large packets of coffee beans, obscuring partially the photographs of Italian soccer stars who seemed to glow munificently like icons above the room, where loners wearing glasses sat and read, and old hippies in rainbow waistcoats, and the young with their elbows propped on the cold laminex tabletops tapped their feet nervously against the legs of their chairs and talked wildly with their hands, while the fans rattled in a whirlpool of smoke.

SCENE 13

Dostoyevsky became aware of the pressure in his side. The floor rolled as he edged his way along the collage of walls to the small cubicle into whose cistern he emptied the contents of his stomach, retching violently. The burning would never have enough. *The knock on the door. His wife washing her hair in the kitchen in the watercolour light. The passage his brother had dug beneath the floor. The knock again, patient and sure. His wife, her head covered by a sheet. It was only on the hill he didn't see the flames he didn't see.*

SCENE 14

The room seemed to vibrate like a beaten drum, music coming from everywhere at once, pawing through the smoke. And behind the counter, in a single candle flame, the woman stood, smiling as she burned.

SCENE 15

Dostoyevsky looked at the ceiling. The noise had stopped. He must have fallen. She leant across his chest, one hand cupped beneath his head, the other holding a glass of water to his lips. Behind her the smoke coiled. He could smell the sweat beneath her arms. He raised himself up on his elbows and drew away from the woman, embarrassed by the intimacy.

SCENE 16

Past midnight and the footpaths were crowded with people, eddying around the small stalls of the fortune tellers and junk wizards. Two ambulancemen were lifting a young man out of the gutter, wiping the vomit from his face and stepping around another who lay bloody in the middle of the road. He hadn't intended going to the club. Saturday nights were the worst. He bought a beer and waited. God climbed out of the froth and stood on the edge of the glass. 'I can see everything, for Christ's sake,' he shouted. 'But I can only judge at the end. You can't blame me for that. Good or bad means nothing here. You're blaming me because the world's not poetry...'

SCENE 17

Dostoyevsky drained his glass. What if God had got it wrong? He made Christ man, but everything Christ did worked; he succeeded in everything, even in death. But to be a man you had to fail.

SCENE 18

The magician walked onto the stage with the hesitancy a hand feels before a flame. His cloak covered everything but his face. A table was lowered from the ceiling and hung before him. Dostoyevsky stopped at the door and turned back to look at him. The magician had slipped his right arm out of its sleeve. For a moment the hand seemed to linger, scarred and accusing. But the motion must have disturbed whatever was holding the table in the air and it came down, pulling the cloak with it as it fell. Almost impossible to watch. The cloak stretched so tight it bent the magician and seemed as if it would fold him in two. But the fabric gave way, tearing at the shoulders and falling. It had happened in an instant, but Dostoyevsky watched as if each frame had been frozen. The naked magician, hands cupped around his genitals.

SCENE 19

He didn't see the face until he was out in the street. He could smell the salt in the air, the sound of men pissing against an alley wall. It was an exultant face. In the moment he had felt his eyes pulled up from the hands, he saw the satisfaction, as if this was what the magician had wanted all along. As if this was the only way he could win. Somehow his failure seemed knowing; he seemed to gain strength from it. When his hands moved over his genitals they were no longer scarred.

SCENE 20

Dostoyevsky knelt by the bed. Outside, in the reserve across the road, he could hear the wild mongrel dreams, random yelps that punctuated the night like falling stars. The city, like a giant whore, opening its legs to the sky.

SCENE 21

A man rides through snow on a bike. Puffs of smoke rise occasionally from the surrounding hills then disappear. A small house can be seen through the white fir trees. It is on fire but does not burn. The man's knees rise and fall through the snow.

SCENE 22

He drifted in and out of sleep, knees aching against the wooden floor.

SCENE 23

A man and a woman sit in a small kitchen drinking tea. The man's hand rests on the woman's leg beneath the table. A cat rubs itself against the man's chair leg. There is a knock on the door, soft and brief. The cat disappears through the window.

SCENE 24

He climbed into the bed, understood. Watching a man
grieve was like watching someone have an orgasm in
public. That was what was so frightening about the
martyrs. Their religious ecstasy was obscene. He'd seen
it, whenever he looked back he saw it, as awful as the
skeletons of the dead rising up out of their graves, the
future, there in the past, its eyes on him, grinning. He sat
on the toilet, his bare feet cold against the tiles. Opened
the window. The night rushed in like an unleashed dog.
The sour sleeping breath of the city. Dostoyevsky woke,
the dawn light frail in his bed as if the world had just
been made and the morning air like a baby's skin, for him
and him alone.

SCENE 25

Vodka burns without smoke. On the stage a woman was
dancing, her breasts bare, her buttocks tense around the
black ribbon that pulled like a harness between her legs.
The men were quiet, drawing absently on cigarettes that
hovered by their mouths. Dostoyevsky's head throbbed
with the light that continued to fall through the stained
glass of his past. The liquid fell through his insides like a
lighted match. He had always been good at spotting charla-
tans smaller than himself, the nocturnal men who loved to
stand on platforms and bay for blood, but what kind of life
was it to call a man a thief before he robbed you?

SCENE 26

The magician, naked except for a loincloth, dragged a giant wooden crucifix into the centre of the room. 'You know me, but not God,' he whispered. 'I know God because I come from Him and He sent me.' Dostoyevsky watched as the big men from the door edged quietly into the room. 'He who eats my flesh and drinks my blood, abides in me and I in him.' Dostoyevsky marvelled at the sheer inappropriateness of it. The bouncers grabbed the naked magician from behind and held him tight by the arms, the cross dropping heavily to the floor. The magician looked directly at Dostoyevsky sitting at the corner of the bar. Pulling his hands free from the men who struggled to hold him he held them up, palms out, for the man to see. Dostoyevsky straightened on the stool. He could see the delicate lace lines as clearly as his own, and in the centre of each palm, the scars of the stigmata. They were much smaller than he imagined them to be.

SCENE 27

It wasn't until he turned his hand over to lift the small saucer that he noticed the scars. The woman anticipated another story. Dostoyevsky bit the inside of his bottom lip. Tonight, he thought, anything was possible. He looked at his palms. 'Hélène, will you sit down with me for a moment?' The woman looked around the café at the empty tables. The streets were quiet, the moon thinning like a cloud. He glanced at the soft roundness of the woman's shirt and thought of the body beneath. 'I don't suppose you've got any whisky?' he said. The woman walked behind the counter, returning with a long bottle and a small glass which she placed on the table in front of the man. 'It's the best I can do,' she said as she leaned in front of him and poured the spirit into the glass.

SCENE 28

Dostoyevsky had never been so close to the tattoo before. He could have touched the woman's shoulder with his lips.

'What happened tonight?'

'Nothing.'

'What did you do to your hands?'

'I saw Him, Hélène.'

The woman laughed, the urgency in the man's voice.

'Please, don't, not tonight...' He saw the magician struggling free. 'Christ has come back.'

The woman laughed again, certain now that the man was playing another of his tricks. No matter how she prepared herself, she was always deceived. 'You shouldn't joke about those kind of things.' She looked at him, her face glowing.

Dostoyevsky wanted more than anything else to doubt himself. He couldn't remember how he had gotten from the club to the café. How could he be sure of anything else? But no matter how many questions he asked, the vision was there: God existed; there was no one left to fight. That was the real pain of martyrdom, surely – to know what by knowing makes faith worthless. He understood now the cunning of God and began to laugh too, abandoning himself to the woman and his own incurable absurdity.

'Stop it, Fyodor, please.'

'But I had you fooled, Hélène.'

SCENE 29

Intoxicated by the revelation, he reached across the table and placed his hand on top of the woman's. She did not move. 'I had a friend in St Petersburg whose father used to sell ice-cream.' With his free hand he poured himself another glass of the sweet spirit. He was smiling at the woman, flushed with happiness. 'On Sundays he'd have to help his father. Every Saturday at school we'd see him praying to God to make it rain. But Sunday was the best day for business. I used to imagine his father praying for the sun and I wondered how, if there was a God, he'd resolve these competing claims...'

SCENE 30

Somewhere in the story the man lost the source of happiness and by the end he could no longer remember why he had started speaking. In the silence that followed the woman withdrew her hand. She collected the bottle and glass and walked back behind the counter. The man couldn't repress the unbearable nostalgia the act produced in him, the hand slipping gently out of his own and the lingering warmth.

He had lived that moment so many times now he had
forgotten how to feel. The arguments he had loved so much
as a young man, his mother's haunted face, the tiny feet of
his wife, and even now, the woman bending over the sink,
her face in the window, partially covered by the café signs
and softened by scarves of steam, the small tattoo rising
up above the neck of her shirt, even now there had been
something close to joy, something hidden in the touch,
hidden like the atoms of the skin, that made him want to
weep, though his mouth could only twitch and his eyelids
quiver.

TRANSLATIONS

*In a late Notebook entry, Paul Ancel (formerly Celan)
attempted the following translation. He had come to view
translation as a shadow that was also, somehow, the light that
threw it; a fire that leaves, like ash in the new language, a
trace of the original...*

es sind
noch Lieder zu singen jenseits
der Menschen

Il était assis dans une petite pièce à Paris et écrivait à la lueur d'une bougie. On devrait s'habituer à l'obscurité, pensa-t-il. Un homme peut passer toute sa vie dans l'obscurité et ne jamais s'y habituer. Il commençait à resentir la même chose pour la lumière. Il éteignit la bougie, mais les mots restèrent devant lui, dans l'obscurité. Comme des cendres, comme une sorte de fantôme. C'était la même chose avec la poésie. Les mots avaient leur façon de survivre.

Sprich –
Doch scheide das Nein nicht vom Ja.
Gib deinem Spruch auch den Sinn:
Gib ihm den Schatten.

Cela faisait trois semaines qu'il essayait de traduire ces mots. Il n'était toujours pas sûr si, même maintenant, il les comprenait; et pourtant il savait ce qu'il écrivait: les mots lui étaient venus comme dans un rêve. Il pensait à sa mère qu'ils avaient tuée d'une balle dans la tête – plus capable de travailler. C'est elle qui parlait ainsi:

Sprich –
Doch scheide das Nein nicht vom Ja.
Gib deinem Spruch auch den Sinn:
Gib ihm den Schatten.

Il avait traduit Blok et Mandelstam, Rimbaud et Valéry, Shakespeare et Emily Dickinson – toutes des victoires à la Pyrrhus, toutes ces horribles heures d'écriture à la lumière d'une bougie éteinte, comme il l'avait dit un jour. Mais tout cela n'était rien à côté de ceci, cette traduction d'allemand en allemand. Il y avait l'incendie et puis après, les cendres.

Dehors, la lumière était comme un saule. Il pouvait sentir l'odeur de la rivière et il se dirigeait rapidement vers elle. Les mots se bousculaient dans sa tête. Un fragment – il y a douze ans? Cela aurait même pu être lui qui parlait de sa vie, avant: *Inmitten all dieser Verluste verblieb das Eine:*

Sprache. Sie, die Sprache, überdauerte, war nicht verloren, ja, trotz
allem. Aber sie musste ihre eigene Antwortlosigkeit durchschreiten,
durch furchtsame Verstummung, durch die tausend Dunkelheiten
todbringender Rede. Sie ging hindurch und gab keine Worte zurück
für das was geschah. Dennoch, sie ging durch dieses Geschehnis.
Ging hindurch und konnte wieder ans Licht kommen, 'bereichert'
von alledem. Il s'était demandé si ce n'était pas seulement lui,
si tous les poèmes n'étaient que des cendres de l'indicible
ou alors, peut-être parfois une façon de passer outre, une
façon d'extirper à mains nues quelque chose des flammes.

Der Fluss dränget sich wie ein Schatten zu seinen
Füßen, ruhig und grau. *He speaks truly who speaks the shade.*
Die Erinnerung ließ ihn innehalten. So hatte er es sich
nie vorgestellt, dass auch Sprache wie ein Mensch war
und das nicht nur weil sie denken konnte, ja in der Tat
zum Denken geboren war; mehr noch, dass auch sie ihre
eigenen Initiationsriten haben muss, und demzufolge ihr
eigenes Heimweh, das dem des Menschen glich und dann
wiederum nicht – sein Exil und sein Geist. Er fragte sich,
ob der große Gott, an den er nicht glauben wollte, jemals
lachte. Dann ließ er sich in die schwarze Milch sinken.

* * * *

there are
still songs to be sung on the other side
*   of mankind*

He sat in a small room in Paris, writing in the light of a candle. One should get used to the dark, he thought. A man could spend his whole life in darkness and never grow used to it. He'd begun to feel the same about the light. He extinguished the candle but the words remained before him in the dark. Like ash, a kind of ghost. It was like that with poetry. Words had a way of surviving.

Speak –
But keep yes and no unsplit.
And give your say this meaning:
Give it the shade.

He'd been trying to translate these words for three weeks. He was not sure that even now he understood them, yet he knew what he would write. The words had come to him as in a dream. He was thinking about his mother whom they had shot in the head – no longer fit for work. The words were hers:

Speak –
But keep yes and no unsplit.
And give your say this meaning:
Give it the shade.

He had translated Blok and Mandelstam, Rimbaud and Valéry, Shakespeare and Emily Dickinson, Pyrrhic victories all of them, those terrible hours writing in the light of the extinguished candle, as he had once put it. But none of that had come even close to this, this translation of the German into German. There was fire, and then there was ash.

Outside, lamplight stood like willow. He could smell the river and he walked briskly towards it. Words rushed his head. A fragment – twelve years ago? It might even have been himself, speaking of the life before: *There remained in the midst of the losses this one thing: language. It, the language, remained, not lost, yes in spite of everything. But it had to pass through its own answerlessness, pass through frightful muting, pass through the thousand darknesses of death-bringing speech. It passed through and gave back no words for that which happened; yet it passed through this happening. Passed through and could come to light again, 'enriched' by all this.* He had wondered then if it wasn't just himself, if all poems were but ashes of the unutterable, and if not that, perhaps at times a *reaching* through, a barehanded snatching from the flames.

The river pushed like shadow at his feet, quiet and grey. *Wahr spricht, wer Schatten spricht.* The memory made him stop. He'd never thought of it like this, that language too was like a man, and that not only because it could think, was born thinking, in fact; but more that that: that it too must have its own rites of passage, and hence its own nostalgia, that was of man yet also somehow not – his exile and his ghost. *Er fragte sich, ob der große Gott, an den er nicht glauben wollte, jemals lachte.* Then lowered himself into the black milk.

SANS

It seemed to me that all language was an excess of language

SAMUEL BECKETT

analogy

perhaps the first sentence

two marionettes pants around their knees in a field churned
to a sea of mud mouths open heads tilted back watching
a bird of prey circling the sky then stop then drop as if
through a gallows of air

they dont see the hare until the bird at the still of its drop
snatches the creature up soundless and is gone

the larger marionette paces makes to think chews his pen
end and stares out at the darkness in which people in silence
sit pauses then takes the smaller marionette by the hand
points at the darkness and then at the vanishing bird of
prey with his pen

in this moment is something of the origin of words he

thinks not that words stand for things but the other way
around the thought in his strings
that the thing might stand for the word

*Now this: your father teaching you to light a match on your
arse. Lighting the old oil lamp in the spilling dark, removing the
white glass globe, then the smoke-blackened inner glass, firing
the wick with the lighted match, or a spill. And your mother
mouthing with closed eyes from her bed how you were born with
the sun behind the larches sinking. This almost silent voice to
which you listen. Down, down to the disaster. Rise now and
disappear.*

gesture
better back better subtract back to the start
the smaller of the two marionettes in thought also thinks
in his words there is something of the origin of these strings
in his words there is something of the trace of what remains
words the smoke words the wood words the ash
silence fire

*Rise now and disappear. A man holding a hand. A woman
holding a hand. Hand holding hand. Everywhere, ash gaining.*

trace
what use to speak here origin of words scribbled in the
throat gone with the breath no trace but the ear it shapes
like a snail its shell bruises and scars language too hard

voice jealous to be heard silence pulls the strings darkness
pulls the strings nothing pulls the strings

'There is a French girl also whom I am fond of, dispassionately,
& who is very good to me. The hand will not be overbid. As we
both know that it will come to an end there is no knowing how
long it may last.' How long it did last...to fill the silence with
sound...rise now and disappear...all ghosts rise...

death
on on all life this search for a language he did not know
could not learn did not exist might not be conceived
imagined dreamed forgotten but a language all the same in
which he might sing without a voice

CURTAIN

What torture it is to cut the nails on your right hand!

CHEKHOV, LETTER TO OLGA KNIPPER,
30 OCTOBER 1903

In a one-room cottage on an enlarged photograph of the hillside above Yalta, the Black Sea dimly audible (wind trapped in a bottle would do), is a table with two legs and half a chair, a curtain for a wall. On the table is the body of a dead man, a coin on each eye. Slowly, a faint light begins to spill through the curtain. By the time it is possible to see the dead man he has faded so badly that nothing remains visible but the hair and eyebrows. And the lorgnette he chooses to wear, even in death. A moth with its right wing missing flits around the folds in the curtain. There is the tapping of a typewriter. An apple hovers just above the chair, as does a long-stemmed flower, dropping petals that do not fall. The moth, the sea, the petals seem almost to make a melody, but far away. As the houselights go up, the room is bathed uselessly in the most beautiful crimson light. No one enters. [Curtain]

Sources

Preface

Elias Canetti, *Kafka's Other Trial: The Letters to Felice,* Harmondsworth, Penguin Books, 1982.

Elias Canetti, *Party in the Blitz,* translated by Michael Hofmann, London, The Harvill Press, 2005.

Things

Italo Calvino, *Invisible Cities*, translated by William Weaver, London, Picador, 1974.

(The epigraph is in fact a quotation from the opening of Ludwig Wittgenstein's *Tractatus Logico-Philosophicus,* translated by C. K. Ogden and F. P. Ramsey, London, Routledge, 1922.)

South

Constantine Cavafy, *Collected Poems*, translated by Edmund Keeley and Philip Sherrard, Princeton, Princeton University Press, 1992.

Herodotus, *The Histories,* translated by Aubrey De Sélincourt, Harmondsworth, Penguin Books, 1954.

Holes

Walter Benjamin, *Illuminations*, translated by Harry Zohn, London, Fontana/Collins, 1982.

Breath

Céleste Albaret, *Monsieur Proust*, as told to Georges Belmont, translated by Barbara Bray, New York, New York Review of Books, 2003.

Walter Benjamin, *Illuminations*, translated by Harry Zohn, London, Fontana/Collins, 1982.

Stone

Osip Mandelstam, *Selected Poems*, translated by Clarence Brown and W. S. Merwin, Oxford, Oxford University Press, 1973.

Nadezhda Mandelstam, *Hope Against Hope: A Memoir*, translated by Max Hayward, New York, The Modern Library, 1999.

Blues

Bob Dylan, *Chronicles: Volume One*, New York, Simon & Schuster, 2004.

Samuel Taylor Coleridge, *Notebooks*, edited by Kathleen Coburn, Merton Christensen and Anthony John Harding (5 Volumes), Princeton, Princeton University Press, 1957–2002.

Boxes

Jodi Hauptman, *Joseph Cornell: Stargazing in the Cinema*, New Haven & London, Yale University Press, 1999.

Disquiet

Fernando Pessoa, *Selected Poems*, translated by Jonathan Griffin, London, Penguin Books, 1982.

Fernando Pessoa, *The Book of Disquiet*, translated by Richard Zenith, London, Penguin Books, 2001.

Bones

Eugenio Montale, *Poems*, edited by Harry Thomas, London, Penguin Books, 2002.

Still

Blaise Pascal, *Pensées*, translated by A. J. Krailsheimer, London, Penguin Books, 1995.

Rags

Rollo H. Myers, *Erik Satie*, New York, Dover Publications, 1968.

Hans Christian Anderson, *The Complete Fairytales*, edited by Lily Owens, New York, Gramercy Books, 1996.

Wrinkles

Fyodor Dostoyevsky, *The Brothers Karamazov*, translated by David Magarshak, Harmondsworth, Penguin Books, 1979.

Ray Monk, *Ludwig Wittgenstein: The Duty of Genius*, London, Vintage, 1991.

Ludwig Wittgenstein, *Notebooks 1914–16*, edited by G. E. M. Anscombe and G. H. von Wright, London, Blackwell, 1961.

Ludwig Wittgenstein, *Tractatus Logico-Philosophicus*, translated by C. K. Ogden and F. P. Ramsey, London, Routledge, 1922.

Ludwig Wittgenstein, *Philosophical Remarks*, edited by Rush Rhees, London, Blackwell, 1975.

Ludwig Wittgenstein, *The Blue and Brown Books*, London, Blackwell, 1975.

Ludwig Wittgenstein, *Philosophical Investigations,* ed. G. E. M. Anscombe and R. Rhees, London, Blackwell, 1953.

Caged

John Cage, *Silence: Lectures and Writings,* London, Calder and Boyars, 1968.

Magic

Fyodor Dostoyevsky, *The Brothers Karamazov*, translated by David Magarshak, Harmondsworth, Penguin Books, 1979.

Translations

Paul Celan, *Selected Poems*, translated by Michael Hamburger, London, Penguin Books, 1995.

Paul Celan, *Selected Poems and Prose of Paul Celan*, translated by John Felstiner, New York, Norton, 2001.

J.M. Coetzee, 'In the Midst of Losses', *The New York Review of Books*, 5 July, 2001.

John Felstiner, *Paul Celan: Poet, Survivor, Jew*, New Haven and London, Yale University Press, 2001.

(The author would like to acknowledge his indebtedness to Inge Stocker, Jose Pavis and Tom Drevikovsky for their assistance in the French and German translations.)

Sans

Samuel Beckett, *Malone Dies*, London, Picador, 1979.

James Knowlson, *Damned to Fame: The Life of Samuel Beckett*, New York, Simon & Schuster, 1996.

Curtain

Jean Benedetti (editor and translator), *Dear Writer, Dear Actress: The Love Letters of Anton Chekhov and Olga Knipper,* New York, Ecco, 1996.

Acknowledgements

Earlier versions of 'South', 'Bones', 'Disquiet', 'Stone' and 'Between' were published in *Stardust: HEAT 9, New Series*, 2005. An earlier version of 'Blindness' was published as 'Untitled' in *Meanjin 4*, 1993. It was also adapted as a stage play and performed in the Studio at the Sydney Opera House as part of the Asian Music & Dance Festival, 2002. An earlier version of 'Things' was published as 'The Library of Lost Things', a catalogue essay for the exhibition *Lost and Found* at the State Library of Victoria, 2005. A version of 'Blues' was published in *Studies in Documentary Film*, 2007.

This project has been assisted by the Commonwealth Government through the Australia Council, its arts funding and advisory body.